SECRETS
UNDER THE SUN

Last Chance Beach

KARI LEMOR

Rycon Press

Secrets Under the Sun © 2021 by Kari Lemor

Cover Art by: Karasel

Photos: depositphoto

RyCon Press

First Electronic Edition: Nov 2021

ISBN - 978-1-954056-10-7

First Print Edition: Nov 2021

ISBN - 978-1-954056-11-4

ALSO BY KARI LEMOR

Sweet and Semi-sweet books

Last Man Standing

Donovan

Last Chance Beach

Secrets Under the Sun

Masquerade Under the Moon

Sounds of Silence

Perfect Silence

Storms of New England novellas

Forgotten Dreams

Sweet Dreams

Rangers of Acadia

Jordan Pond

Sassy and spicy books

Storms of New England (small town)

Elusive Dreams	-	True Dreams
Stolen Dreams	-	Broken Dreams
Lost Dreams	-	Faded Dreams

Love on the Line (light suspense)

Wild Card Undercover	-	Running Target
Fatal Evidence	-	Hidden Betrayal
Death Race	-	Tactical Revenge

Acknowledgements

I have many people to thank on this journey. My husband and children who give me all their love and support. Kris and Meredith for so much support and encouragement, even when you are short on time yourself. Especially to Em, who has been the best editor I've ever had, giving me suggestions, guidance, and so much assistance making my books super shiny. To Donna for the honest feedback and excellent suggestions. To all the Gems authors who encourage and share my books with others. To all the amazing readers who have left reviews letting me know I have a purpose in writing. And to the other Last Chance Beach authors who also believe in Island Magic.

This book is dedicated to everyone who loves the beach.
There's nothing better than the wind and the waves to bring peace to
our lives.

CHAPTER ONE

"They've done it again."

Konstantine Petrakis ran his hands through his hair as he listened to his younger brother over the phone. "What was it this time?"

"The marketing logo and logline for the weekend getaway package. Almost exactly word for word. If we put ours out now, the logo is similar enough to be noticed."

"Didn't we trademark our logo? We can take them to court."

Demitrius cleared his throat. "We still hadn't finalized the logo, so we hadn't put in for the trademark yet."

Konstantine pounded his fist on his desk and clenched his teeth. "We need to find out who's doing this, Trey," he said. Konstantine and Demitrius had taken forever to yell out when they were younger, so they'd become Dean and Trey.

"Yeah, I was thinking the same thing. I don't know who to trust there. Hugh has been at the resort for years, but he wasn't too pleased when we hired Aarya as the manager instead of promoting him."

"Did he tell you he was upset? Why is this the first I'm hearing of it?"

Dean was president and CEO of Yios Corporation that owned and managed a dozen luxury oceanfront hotels and resorts around the world. Trey was his equal partner, vice president, and the CFO. Trey was the face of Yios, while Dean preferred to stay in his home office and run things remotely. It had been that way since their father passed away over ten years ago when Dean was only thirty-two. Vasileios Petrakis had started the company back when the boys were little, so they'd grown up learning the business from the ground floor up. Literally. They'd worked in housekeeping, registration, accounting, marketing, and even did lifeguard and towel boy duties over the summers.

"I didn't hear it from him. Reva mentioned it last time I went down there. She said it on the QT, so I didn't talk to him about it. Maybe I should."

"No, don't accuse him of anything until we have more solid evidence. This is the fourth time we've had The Sands jump our plans. Once, maybe it's a coincidence. Marketing for a beach resort all fits in a similar category. But four times they come up with the exact new promotion we've been working on? Someone wants The Ocean Pearl Resort to be second on the island."

"The best bet would be to get someone inside to snoop around," Trey suggested.

Dean tapped his fingers on his desk. "Do we still have that detective agency on retainer? Maybe they have someone to send who can figure out this mess."

"Mm," Trey hummed. "They're great for checking out new employees, but I think this needs a personal touch. Who knows if it's at the level of the Pearl or if it goes up to corporate? What do you think? A little sun and sand?"

"I don't think you'd blend in too well down there. The staff all know you. You visit at least a half dozen times a year." And Trey usually came back with stories of how many women he'd scored.

"Oh, no, dear brother, I wasn't suggesting I go there. I thought perhaps you'd like to come down from your gated castle and enjoy a few months in the sun. Your olive skin is looking quite pale lately."

"Me? I don't really blend in either." For a completely different reason. As he glanced at the window beside him, the scar that ran down the side of his face pulsed to life. Well, not literally, but it felt like it.

"Oh, please. You simply don your Dean Peters disguise, and no one will ever know you're the wealthy Konstantine Petrakis, mystery owner of Yios Corporation."

Dean hated the fact his brother knew of the alter ego he'd made up when he wanted to slip by and go unnoticed. He'd made sure to stay out of the limelight his whole life. Trey loved that job, and Dean gave it to him with pleasure. But every now and then, he had to make an appearance at the corporate headquarters. The khaki uniform pants and shirt with a cap on his head was never looked at twice. Not when he hadn't shaved in a week.

"You know I don't like being out in public. It's not a good plan."

"It's a great plan, Dean," Trey said. "You need to get over this idea that people see you as less than you are. So you have a scar and a limp. Big deal. Lots of people have them, and they don't stop their lives because of it."

Dean took a deep breath before he responded. "I've hardly stopped my life. I work ten hours a day in the office keeping this business going."

Trey's sigh could be heard across the line. "I know you work hard, but you need to get out of your gilded cage and live a little. It's not healthy for you to stay by yourself all the time."

"I get out now and then. I go down to the Greek deli for lunch sometimes and to the Athena pub once or twice a month."

"Yeah, I've gone with you. You sit on a bar stool, have two beers, maybe say hi to the bartender, then go back home. Hardly the social event of the season."

"I don't need to be social. I've got plenty of money, and I can do whatever I want."

"But you don't, Dean. You don't go anywhere or do anything or spend any of your money. I hate seeing you all by yourself. You need to have some fun. Stop being such a Scrooge all the time. Find a nice girl and have a good time."

"Nice girls don't have the kind of good time you're referring to. And just because I'm not having sex on a daily basis like my playboy younger brother, doesn't mean I don't partake at times."

"This is the perfect opportunity for you to participate even more. Go to Last Chance Beach. I'll set you up with a job there as Dean Peters, and you can work your way through some of the island girls. There're a few I can recommend to show you a little fun. In the meantime, you can do some snooping and figure out who's been leaking our marketing strategies to our rival resort."

Dean clenched his hand around the phone and gritted his teeth. They did have to find the culprit, and Trey was too well known on the island. While Dean had visited twice, he'd never stayed at the resort and hadn't introduced himself to anyone there. He liked his anonymity.

Could he do this? Sure, he could. It would be like a mini vacation for him. But what position would be least noticeable? Not front desk clerk or anything in management. It had to be something no one paid any attention to.

His gaze fell to the wastebasket under his desk. It was emptied every day, and he never thought about who did it. The maintenance staff moved about easily, and most people ignored them. It was perfect.

"I'll do it. Make arrangements for Dean Peters to be transferred from one of the other resorts to the Ocean Pearl in the maintenance department. He'll need a place to live. Nothing fancy or on the beach. There're a few older houses that rent rooms on that street behind the library. Something near that would be good. And I'll need an old truck to use. I think the maintenance guy would be a tad conspicuous driving a BMW."

"Perfect. I'll make the arrangements myself. With the college students going back to school next week, there should be a few holes to fill. And Dean...?"

"What?"

"I know you're going there for a purpose, but maybe take in a little sun, surf, and sand while you're there."

"Sure, why not." *After* he'd caught the person sharing their marketing strategies.

Eleni Griffin finished typing the e-mail, double-checked it for spelling and accuracy, CCed Aarya Lanka, her boss, then hit send. One more item off her ever-growing list of things she hadn't planned on today. At least Aarya was pleasant and thanked her for her time and effort.

The outer door to the management office opened. Hugh Tomlin walked in and waved at Aarya's door. "Is she in?"

"She's currently meeting with Chef in the banquet hall kitchen."

Hugh rolled his eyes and huffed. "Tell her I need to see her ASAP." He spun and was out of the room in seconds, leaving the door wide open.

"Of course, I will, sir. Anything you say, sir. Oh, and you're so very welcome. I'm happy to help you any time I can." Yeah, Aarya was much easier to work for. Unfortunately, The Ocean Pearl Resort only had one administrative assistant for both the manager and assistant manager. She was it.

As she jotted down a note for Aarya about Hugh, a shuffling from the doorway had her looking up. A man in the standard black pants and light blue Ocean Pearl polo shirt stood there, empty trash bag in hand. She'd never seen him before.

Rising, she greeted him. "Hi, I'm Eleni Griffin. Slave labor for the higher ups here. I'm assuming you're new. The training must have finished then."

The man tugged on the brim of his matching Ocean Pearl hat and nodded. The hats weren't required uniform, but some of the employees liked them if their jobs took them outside in the sun often.

"Dean." His voice was low and gruff, but pleasant.

"Dean. Nice to meet you, Dean. What's your position here? I'm sorry. I know I should have memorized all the new staff and their jobs, but it's been hectic with the college students leaving and having to find new replacements."

"Maintenance." His eyes stayed on the floor. Not much of a talker, apparently.

"Wonderful. I assume Santos gave you a tour of the place." Their facilities manager took his responsibility very seriously and would have already given out instructions to the new staff, no doubt.

"Yes, ma'am."

"Did you need something in the office, or are you here for the trash?"

"Just the trash." He held up the bag.

"Fine. Both Aarya and Hugh are out of their offices for the moment, so go on in. It was nice meeting you. I'm sure I'll see you around."

He tipped his head and shuffled past her into Hugh's office. As she sat back at her desk in the outer office, she couldn't help but notice Dean's gait. It was slightly off. Had he hurt himself recently or did he always limp? She certainly wouldn't ask him today. He already seemed withdrawn enough.

She ran her finger down her planner, checking for her next task. Noises drifted out from Hugh's office, and a few minutes later, Dean exited and went into Aarya's office. When he came out, the bag almost full, he stopped and stared at her.

"Do you need something, Dean?"

"Is there trash in this room, too?"

"Oh, I'm sorry, yes. It's behind my desk. Right there." She pointed to her small wastebasket, brimming with paper and pencils shavings. What could she say? She liked her pencils sharp.

Dean shuffled past her desk to reach the barrel, and she finally got a good look at him under his cap. Strong features, probably late thirties or so. A bit of gray peeked out at his temples among otherwise dark hair. Not that she could see much of it with his hat on.

He was tall and lean, but his arms and chest had good definition and filled out the polo shirt nicely. She had to remind herself he was a new employee, and she shouldn't be gawking.

When he turned after emptying her wastebasket, he ducked his head again. A scar ran from his temple down the side of his cheek and disappeared into the scruff on his chin. Was he embarrassed by it? It hardly detracted from his handsome face. She had to admit it had been a while since she'd felt any kind of flutter in the presence of a good-looking guy. The resort constantly had them, all ages, and occasionally they hit on her if she was out of the office. But fraternizing with the guests was a big no-no. For her, anyway. Guests were here short term. No sense in getting to know any of them as more than guests.

"Thank you, Dean. From now on, don't feel you need to ask permission to come in. As long as Aarya or Hugh aren't in the middle of a meeting with someone, just go right in."

"Great." He tied the bag and glanced around.

"If you have any questions or need anything, let me know. I'm happy to help. I'm sure once you've been here a while, it'll all be easier. I'm here Monday, Wednesday, Friday from seven in the morning to six at night, and Saturday until two."

That made him tilt his chin up. And those eyes. Deep brown with full lashes surrounding them. They were gorgeous. Her stomach fluttered, and she held her hand there to try and calm it.

"Those are strange hours."

She cocked her head. "They work for me and for the resort." The three twelve-hour days, with a half day Saturday, made it easier for homeschooling her kids. She loved the island, but one negative was no school here. There was talk of building one, but the plans had been put on hold due to piles of red tape. For now, the kids who lived on Last Chance Beach had to be bused to the mainland. When Xander and Thea started high school, maybe even junior high, she might consider it, but for now she didn't want them having the long bus ride over the bridge.

His mouth tightened, and he nodded again. "Right. Thanks."

"Thank you, Dean. And I meant what I said. If you have any questions or forget something you were supposed to do, let me know. I'm happy to help."

He gazed at her strangely with those beautiful eyes that were so dark, they were almost black. A woman could get lost in them.

"Thank you, Miss, uh, Mrs. Griffin?"

She laughed but appreciated his trying to be accurate. "Eleni is fine. I'll see you later."

"Bye."

As he walked out the door, Eleni took the opportunity to stare at him again. A little older than her perhaps and not hard on the eyes. Too bad his demeanor seemed on the subdued side. Then again, who knew what kind of crap he had in his background? She had her own stuff to deal with.

But wouldn't it be nice to have a conversation with a handsome man and dream of what could happen? Yeah. Dreams were great, but unfortunately, Dean didn't seem to be much of a conversationalist.

CHAPTER TWO

*D*ean walked down the hallway and dumped the trash bag into the pushcart he'd been given earlier at the training. God, if that hadn't been the most excruciating thing he'd ever sat through, he didn't know what was. Two days of listening to the history of the Ocean Pearl and Yios Corporation and how it had gotten started, then hours of strict rules and regulations that all employees had to follow. He already knew all of them. He'd written most of them. What the hell had he been thinking?

Most of the trainings were common sense stuff and how to deal with guests at the resort. As maintenance, he hoped not to really interact with any of them. Or any of the staff either. He wanted to blend into the background and quickly figure out who was giving away their marketing plans.

He hadn't counted on the admin assistant trying to chat him up. Okay, maybe she was only being friendly, but he'd wanted to get in, look around, then get out. With her there, it had been empty the trash and get out. With her working until six at night, it would be difficult for him to take a look around the offices. His snooping would be limited to Tuesday and Thursday.

Eleni Griffin. Thinking back, he remembered skimming her employee report but couldn't recall exactly what hers had said. With a few hundred staff at this resort alone, who could blame him? But working in the management office, she'd have access to any plans being brought up in marketing or promotions.

Her sarcastic words after Hugh had huffed out of the office made him chuckle. Yet it was also disrespectful, and she'd made that joke about being slave labor. Did she really feel that way? Enough to want payback against her employer? He'd have to keep his eye on her.

That thought wasn't an unpleasant one. Eleni was quite pretty with her dark hair, sleek and shiny, that stopped just under her chin. She'd tucked it behind her ears once or twice during the short time he'd been in the office. He hadn't expected her to speak to him or offer him assistance. She was management. Well, kind of. He depended on his admin assistant to do all the little stuff he never had time for and knew he couldn't live without her. Fortunately, she had agreed to work from his house, since he hated going into the corporate office. While he was gone, she was taking care of everything remotely. His new apartment was small, but he'd made sure it had great internet.

Where did Eleni live? And why was he even still thinking of her? *Because she's a suspect.* And she'd treated him with respect today. It was more than the trainer had done or some of the other staff who seemed too high and mighty to talk to maintenance. Even Hugh had stormed past him without even glancing his way. If only these people knew who he was, they would have been falling all over him to make a good impression.

Stupid thought. He needed everyone to ignore him, so he could find evidence of their culprit. Everyone, except Eleni. He didn't want her to ignore him. She'd worn a figure-hugging pair of pants that showcased her curves nicely. Curves a man couldn't help but notice—even one with as much self-control as he had. However, it wasn't a good idea to get involved with employees, no matter what his brother suggested.

Pushing the trash-filled cart down the hallway, he mentally checked off what Santos had given him to do. Not much today. Mostly, learning the layout of the place by emptying the trash in the offices, registration area, banquet and conferences rooms, and other public areas. The chambermaids took care of trash in the individual hotel rooms.

As he approached the largest of the banquet halls, an attractive blonde rushed out of one of the smaller rooms, the Emerald if he recalled correctly. Her four-inch heels clicked rapidly on the tiles as she waved at him.

"Oh, hey, you, whatever your name is. I need you in here immediately." She pivoted abruptly and marched back inside.

It wasn't part of what he was supposed to do today, but she wore a resort name tag, so obviously worked here. He followed her, dragging the cart in behind him. He'd been told he shouldn't leave the trash cart hanging around for any length of time, and he had no idea who this lady was or what she wanted him to do.

Impatience flashed on her perfectly made-up face, and her arms crossed her abundant chest. She waved her hand again and scowled. "We had a bit of a mess when some people cut across the room after being on the beach. I have a business meeting scheduled in here in an hour. We can't set up the tables until the sand is vacuumed up. Can you see to that right away?"

"Um, sure. Where's the vacuum for this part of the resort?"

Her head shook back and forth, her eyes grew wide, and her fingers spread apart like she was ready to lunge for a volleyball headed her way. "How do you not know where the vacuum is? Aren't you maintenance?"

He shuffled his feet and cleared his throat. "Sorry, ma'am, but today's my first day. Well, second, but I was in training until an hour ago."

Her breath huffed out and her eyes narrowed. "And they didn't train you where all the vacuums were?"

"There's a map with that information, but it's back at my locker." He didn't think he'd need it today, since he was only on trash duty. He'd planned to study it tonight once he got back to his apartment.

Her face hardened, and she took a deep breath like she was trying not to scream. "There's a utility room around the corner on the right. I believe there's one in there. You do have a key for that, don't you?" Her voice trumpeted her annoyance.

"Yes. I'll get it right away, ma'am."

He'd caught site of her name tag as he left. Reva Buchinsky. The Activities Director. The woman Trey had insisted they give this job to. Yeah, he could see why his brother wanted to keep her handy. Maybe the reason he liked coming to this resort more than any of the others they owned. Reva looked at least ten years younger than Trey, and it sounded like she was an easy fling whenever he decided to drop in. She was beautiful...on the outside. Certainly nothing like Eleni on the inside, with her authentic smile and understanding of his newbie status.

After finding the correct utility room and pushing the industrial strength vacuum back to the Emerald Room, he plugged it in and started to clean up the wayward sand. The rest of the staff bustled about rearranging tables and chairs, completely ignoring him. Good, that's exactly what he was hoping for.

Now, if he could manage to find who was sabotaging the resort, he could get out of this godforsaken cheery place and go back to his quiet life in the city.

He spent the next few hours finishing up with the trash as well as a few so-called emergencies that popped up along the way. Okay, the vomit from an inebriated guest was definitely an emergency, but he wasn't sure why it was imperative for him to run around the facility trying to find a gold-colored trash can when there were dozens of black ones sitting nearby. In his role as maintenance, it wasn't his job to ask why.

His shift ended at five, yet at six, he was still pushing a broom around the lobby. Wouldn't hurt to suck up to the boss and see who was hanging around the offices. He maneuvered his way down the hall and peeked into the manager's suite.

Eleni stood by her desk, stuffing papers into a tote bag. When he accidentally bumped into the door, she jumped and swung toward him.

"Oh, Dean, I didn't realize you were there. Shouldn't you be done by now?"

Did she seem nervous? She kept glancing at the clock, then toward Aarya's office. What had she been putting in the bag? Was there any way to get a look at it?

"A few emergencies put me behind in my list."

Her face relaxed as she dropped a small purse into her bag, then slung it over her shoulder.

"That's really sweet of you to stay, but I don't think they expect that of you, especially on the first day. You should check with Santos tomorrow and ask what protocol is for your scheduled work when you get pulled into other duties."

"I'll do that. Do you need me for anything?" Could he somehow bump into her and have the bag fall so he could see what was inside?

Her face softened as she stepped toward him. "I appreciate the offer, but it's all good here. I'm just ready to get home and see my kids before they go to bed. Good night."

Kids? She had kids. Which probably meant she had a husband somewhere nearby, too. Why did that bother him? It shouldn't. She was a suspect. Possibly. He was only here to figure out this problem.

He stared at the floor again and nodded. "Good night."

As she walked out the door, he realized he'd been so distracted by her having kids, he'd forgotten he wanted a peek in her bag. Didn't matter. He should probably take a little time to really get to know the building and the everyday workings here. He owned the place, after all. Getting to the bottom of the marketing leaks didn't have to be his only task. While he was here, he could see what ran well and what could be improved upon, who could be promoted and who was dead weight. Yeah, being ignored by everyone was a benefit that would allow him to see people in their true form.

Goal number two. Get to know the staff better. He thought of Eleni and strangely wished she didn't have a family waiting for her at home.

"Mom, Thea took my toast."

Eleni glanced over at her eight-year-old son and sighed. Couldn't they have one morning where it wasn't a struggle to get out of the house?

"Anthea, give Xander back his toast, please."

"She already licked it," Xander whined.

"He stuck boogers on *my* toast, so I took his."

Xander's chuckle gave away what he'd done to his twin sister's breakfast.

Closing her eyes, Eleni took a deep breath and counted to ten. The kids knew this was a red flag and stopped their ruckus immediately. When she opened her eyes again, they had cleaned up their plates and were hopping around, getting shoes on.

"We're taking the bikes today, so no sandals. You need sneakers with socks. Hurry. Nadine will be here with Livy and Kandra any minute."

"Why do we have to leave so early?" Thea pouted as she kicked off her sandals and grabbed sneakers.

"Because the Welcome Center gets very busy later in the morning, and if we want Trudy to answer the questions you have, then we need to go before the tour buses get here."

It was Xander's turn to pout. "Why do tour buses have to come here? Why can't they leave us alone?"

Eleni filled her small, soft-sided lunch box with sandwiches and stuffed it in her backpack. "If tour buses and tourists didn't come to Last Chance Beach, then I wouldn't have a job, and we couldn't live on the island."

"Oh," the twins said in unison. It always freaked her out when they did that. Which was often. Evidently, nine months in the womb practically attached to each other got you synced to the same wavelength.

For good measure, she added, "And if we didn't live on the island, you'd be inside a school building on this beautiful day, instead of home-schooled and spending the day outside with your studies."

Her children cheered and danced around the kitchen. Eleni rolled her eyes, then headed to the door as a horn beeped in the driveway.

Livy and Kandra jumped out of Nadine's minivan and scurried into the house to find their friends.

Nadine laughed and leaned on the open window. "They were so excited about spending the day looking through the tide pools. I almost couldn't get them to sleep last night. You always do the coolest field trips."

"Because I teach them science. I'm so glad you take the math lessons, because if I did, these kids would be failing, big time."

She and Nadine worked together to homeschool the four children. Eleni always felt guilty that Nadine did three days of studies while she only did two. She tried to make up for it by taking the girls overnight if both Nadine, who worked as a dispatcher, and her husband, Marek, who worked at the Island Rescue, had to do overlapping shifts. It wasn't often, but it gave Nadine peace of mind to have somewhere for her girls to go.

It also made the small, three-bedroom house kind of squishy at times.

"You throw in plenty of math during your trips. Kandra's always complaining when you do. Gotta run. Bert gets cranky if he can't get out of his shift right at seven."

Eleni waved as Nadine drove away toward the coast where the Rescue dispatch was housed. Glancing at her watch, she calculated how long it would take to bike over to the Welcome Center, then counted back. They had a few minutes before they needed to leave. Maybe she could sneak in another cup of coffee.

When she entered the house, the girls sat in the living room admiring the bright red polish Livy had on her nails.

"Hey, Kandra, you got your locs retwisted. Looks good."

Kandra shook her head and beamed. Livy glared at her older sister and looked back at her nails. "Dad got his redone, too. Mom and I just got our nails done." Livy had softer spiral curls like their mother, while Kandra took after their dad. Thea often sulked that her hair was pin straight and boring. The grass was always greener somewhere else.

"Do you girls need anything to eat before we go? We'll be spending an hour or so at the Welcome Center doing research on the history of the island. Then, we'll head down to the beach. Low tide should be right around nine this morning, and hopefully we'll be able to find all sorts of creatures in the tidal pools. I've packed measuring cups in your backpacks, and we'll be comparing units of measurement with both solid and liquid. We'll spend a half hour journaling our findings, then have lunch."

"Can we eat at the Pearl?" Xander asked, shoving a water bottle into his bag.

She shrugged. "Depends on how busy it is. If there aren't too many people down by the docks, we might be able to use one of their tables. But we're not buying anything at the snack shack. I brought sandwiches, and you all have snacks in your bags."

Thea made a face. The girl knew the snacks were healthy ones and not the sugar-filled junk she loved to eat. Eleni would try and make cookies this weekend if she managed to get to the grocery store off island in the next few days. The groceries at the small store here were just too darn expensive to buy all the time.

"Make sure you've got everything in your bags and head out to the bikes. I need to let YiaYia know I'm leaving."

As the kids bounced toward the door, Eleni trotted down the hall to her mother's room. Georgina Matsoukas had come to live with them three years ago when her hearing had started to fade due to a viral infection. Before that, she'd helped Eleni with the kids after Sean had died. She still helped on Saturdays when Eleni worked and during the late afternoons before she got home. Now that the children were a little older, she didn't worry as much because she knew Thea and Xander were able to use the phone if an emergency arose.

She opened the door to her mother's room and flicked the light switch. Mom glanced up from her iPad, the one extravagance Eleni had insisted on, and smiled.

"Are you leaving now?"

Eleni nodded and signed *yes*. She and the kids had been learning American Sign Language over the last few years and teaching her mom. The woman still had clear speech but couldn't always get what was said by reading lips.

Eleni spoke and signed at the same time. "*School at the beach today. Library after lunch. Do you need anything?*"

Mom laughed. "I wish I had school like that when I was little. Have fun. I'm just fine."

Eleni kissed Mom on the cheek and took off down the hall to grab her bag. Her mom had only just turned sixty and was still healthy in all other ways, but she still worried.

Outside, she climbed on her bike, checked to make sure all helmets were securely fastened, then started peddling. It was maybe a twenty-minute ride from their house to the Welcome Center, and on a beautiful day like today, they all enjoyed it. The tourist crowd was still heavy in early September due to warm temperatures, but since school had started not as many families with kids showed up during the week.

At the Welcome Center, Trudy happily answered all the questions the kids had for her. Their assignment last week had been to write an e-mail and send it to her so she could have time to look up any information she didn't know. Which wasn't much. Trudy had spent her entire seventy-two years on this island and bragged she'd only left for two occasions in her life.

Eleni listened as the woman dramatically retold the legend of Last Chance Beach and how the island got its name. They'd heard it at least a dozen times, but the way Trudy told it, it never got old.

Eleni loved the story of the young woman who had waited for many years to find a perfect love. But when an impoverished young man entered her life, she felt as if they'd always known each other. Her wealthy father, seeing his daughter's infatuation, ordered the young man to be imprisoned in the hold of a ship that was leaving port the next day. Then, he locked his daughter in her room to keep her away from him. The daughter schemed and bribed until she could run away to the land her beloved had told stories of. But he wasn't there. She searched from town to town, until she finally made it to an island not far from the mainland. A minister and his wife invited her to stay with them. However, they had one other guest who had escaped from a ship and been battered by the ocean's waves. When the young man came down to dinner, limping along on crutches, she ran into his arms. It was the man she'd fallen in love with. Fate had provided them with one last chance to find each other.

Eleni wandered around the center as the children asked more questions and jotted down notes. They knew they'd have to journal about this visit before lunch. As she gazed out the window, the activity at The Ocean Pearl Resort next door caught her attention. Tuesdays weren't a super busy day. Anyone staying for a week typically checked in either Sunday or Monday and checked out Friday or Saturday. Weekend guests were either Thursday or Friday check ins.

A figure in the black pants, blue shirt uniform caught her attention. Tall, trim but athletic-looking, and the ball cap on his head. He was weed whacking around the side of the building. Was it Dean, the new maintenance guy? No one else in that department had the same build.

Eleni started humming, then scolded herself. She knew nothing about the man other than what his resume and application said. Yes, she'd peeked. It was part of her job to know every one of the staff, nothing more.

His file wasn't very informative. Apparently, he'd worked at one of the other Yios resorts on Cape Cod. There was no reason listed for why he'd transferred, and his personal information was limited. They didn't necessarily require many personal details about him, but it was always nice to have some information so you didn't make a gaff when chatting.

Like all the people who asked about the kids' father. Many assumed she was divorced or had never been married when they met her. She'd taken her wedding ring off several years ago, knowing she'd needed to move on. She hadn't. Not really. She'd gone out to dinner occasionally with some of the locals, but nothing had ever come of it. Taking on two ready-made kids, and now her mother, wasn't something many guys wanted to deal with. Her life was full between work and home, so she didn't like to dwell on it.

She shouldn't be dwelling on the fine figure of Dean Peters either. He'd barely said two sentences to her yesterday and had kept his eyes lowered almost the entire time. Maybe, eventually, she could get him more comfortable with her and the other staff.

The kids running across the room got her attention, so she slid back into teacher mode and gave them directions on the next activity. Xander had asked to eat at the resort, and she rarely went back there when she wasn't working. Glancing out the window again at a tall, handsome maintenance worker gave her a little push to perhaps allow Xander his wish. It had nothing to do with Dean Peters.

CHAPTER THREE

*H*e wasn't imagining things. That was Eleni on the bike, peddling down the walkway toward the beach. Four kids trailed behind her. He thought he'd seen her earlier in the day in the Welcome Center parking lot, but from this distance, he couldn't be sure. Now, he was.

He finished pushing the broom across the tennis court and took a closer look. Were all those her kids? Two of them had her dark, silky hair and olive tone, but the other two had curlier hair and darker skin. Of course, he had no idea what her husband looked like.

He shouldn't even be thinking about her, yet as a possible suspect, he couldn't ignore anything she did. Maybe it was time to empty the trash on the patio near the beach. He'd done it two hours ago, but that area typically needed to be redone often.

The fact it was only his second day on the job—training didn't count—and he already knew the fill rate of each trashcan was weird. He gave another once over of both tennis courts and sighed. A guest had complained about some rocks on the surface, so he'd been sent out here to fix the problem. How did maintenance ever get any of their routine work done when they were called to "emergencies" a few times an hour? He and Trey might need to rethink staffing for that department. They'd left it up to the management of each property, yet if he was run ragged in only two days, what happened to these staff members after months or years. Might account for some of the turnover rate.

After returning the broom to the correct closet, he grabbed his cart and a roll of trash bags and pushed along the paved path. Eleni and the kids sat on the grassy area next to the volleyball court and horseshoe pits on the beach. She sat on a bench while the kids reclined on the grass, and they each had a sandwich in their hands.

He whistled a few tuneless notes as he approached the cans near her, and she looked up. Her face beamed with pleasure, and Dean was frozen in place for a second. He didn't think he'd ever had someone look at him that way. Not with real joy on her face. Several women who'd known of his wealth had attempted something similar, but he could sniff out fake from a mile away.

"Hi, Dean. How's the second day coming along?"

He'd love to sit and chat and get to know her better, but it wasn't the right time, and he needed to be as unobtrusive as possible.

"Busy." He got to work with the trash. Before he tied up the bags, Eleni jumped up and waved at the kids.

"Hey, get everything you need to throw away and do it now, so we don't waste any more bags."

"Okay, Mom," the boy in the group called out and barreled over to slam dunk his wrappers. Several fell out of the bag onto the ground.

Eleni scowled. "Xander, pick those up. Dean isn't paid to clean up after you."

The boy looked sheepish, got the trash, and carefully stuck it inside the bag. "Sorry, Mr. Dean. I'm Xander. This is my mom. She works here, too."

"I know. I met her yesterday. Thanks for picking that up."

"No problem."

The kid got a goofy look on his face and stared at Dean. Most likely, checking out his scar. Lowering his head, he shook the bag to get the contents to shift and settle. The girls strode over and deposited their wrappers, each thanking him. It was good to know Eleni had taught them manners.

"Dean, these are my children, Thea and Xander. And these other lovely ladies are Kandra and Livy. Their mother and I share homeschooling duties."

"Hmm, so the weird schedule..."

She nodded. "Yup, and it works for the resort, because Saturday is the busiest day here. There's lots to do."

"Seems like there's lots to do every day."

Eleni laughed, and the sound was musical. It swept through him, making him forget he'd been picking up trash all day.

"It's still the busy season. Once the temps go down a bit, we'll see a decline in guests. We're never completely empty, since *our* cold season is still warm compared to those who live up north. But it's not quite so crazy."

"Good to know." Mostly because it meant he and Trey needed to work with the marketing department to find other ways to get people here in those cooler months. Except they had someone who kept sharing their marketing with a rival resort.

Eleni took a sip from her water bottle and a few drops splashed onto her chin. Her skin flushed a pretty pink, and she turned away to wipe it off. "Sorry, I'm not the most graceful person on this planet."

He wanted to tell her she absolutely was, but he pushed the comment back and looked down again. "Are you all done with your trash?" He held the bag open and glanced around. It really was a beautiful spot. The sounds of the ocean did something to relax him, even with the crappy jobs he'd been doing.

"It's nice here. I hope you'll like it. Where did you live before this?"

He had to stop and think what had been on his application. The truth was always good. Part of it, anyway. "I lived just south of Boston, near Cape Cod."

Her smile showcased the dimple in one cheek. "You wanted something a little warmer, huh?"

He nodded, not wanting to lie to her. Sure, he was lying to everyone here, including the managers. Why should he feel bad about doing it with one admin assistant? Because she'd been nice to him.

"Well, we need to get back to our studies. It was nice seeing you again, Dean. Are you working tomorrow?"

"Yeah. Diving in with both feet."

"I'll see you then. Make sure to enjoy the island once you get off work. If you aren't sure where to go, check in with me, and I'll give you some suggestions of great places to eat or hang out."

"Appreciate it." Not that he planned to start having a social life simply because he moved here. Doubtful the locals knew who was sharing their marketing plans, so why get to know them?

"Let's go, kids," Eleni called out. "Make sure to check that we aren't leaving any trash on the ground.

The children made a game of running around the grassy area, then picked up their backpacks and shrugged them on. Xander wandered over to him and stuck out his hand. "It was nice to meet you, Mr. Dean. I hope I get to see you again soon. Do you play basketball? 'Cause, if you do, we've got a hoop on our street. It's not ours, but the guy next door lets us use it sometimes. Can you come play?"

Dean shook his hand and tipped his head. He wasn't sure how to respond to the question. The kid's dad wouldn't want him sniffing around the house if he knew how attracted he was to Eleni.

"Xander, time to go. Let Dean get his work done." Eleni threw him another winning smile. Why did it shake something loose inside him?

He knew he should get back to work as Eleni and the kids rode off, but he was rooted to the spot until they were completely out of sight.

It wasn't until after his shift had ended, and he was doing a last check of trash in the admin offices, that Dean had a chance to peek in the employee files. Aarya had started early today, so Hugh was working the later shift. But Hugh, as Dean had noticed in only a few days, liked to walk around the pool area during his shift. Luckily, it left the office empty so he could snoop around.

The filing cabinet with the staff info was locked, but Trey had given him keys to everything in the building. Even though there were plenty of possible suspects, Dean focused this trip on Eleni's file. He'd read what was in her electronic file last night, but that was nothing more than her application from five years ago, her education, and her salary history. Often, personal notes were placed in the paper files at the specific resort.

After peeking out the window in the outer office, and assuring himself Hugh was still by the pool, Dean flipped through Eleni's file. All great notes on her excellent work ethic. As he finished the last sheet, one note caught his attention. She'd taken a few weeks off, and they had paid her even though she hadn't earned the time yet.

Her husband had died. Five years ago. God, the kids must have been very young at the time. She'd been raising them by herself all this time. Part of him wondered if she needed the money. Was it enough that she'd sell secrets to buy what she needed for the kids? Her address was only a street over from him, and most of the houses there were on the small side. Doubtful she was living the high life, not with her salary.

As he carefully returned her file to the correct place, he thought about her situation. Today, when he'd met her children, he'd stayed distant like he always did when near kids. But Xander had reached out to him as a friend, and Thea had given him a sweet smile very like her mother's. It was sad they didn't have a father. He felt like a jerk for the tiny bit of relief that had hit him when he'd learned Eleni wasn't married.

The click of Reva's heels had Dean holding his breath. Was she planning to ream him out about something else or send him on a wild goose chase yet again? The woman seemed to think he was her personal servant. He didn't mind when it was clear it was an errand for the resort, but he had a feeling a few of the trips he made to the post office or town hall to deliver things were more because she was lazy and didn't want to run out herself.

Ducking into the storage closet, he peeked out as she strode by. Must be his lucky day, because she didn't stop to accost him with ridiculous demands for the activities she'd planned. From what he understood of the management of this resort, she had staff specifically for scheduled activities. Maintenance could be used for set up and cleaning but shouldn't be taken from their daily tasks for hers.

Once she'd passed by and was well out of sight, he headed to the elevator to start vacuuming the guest floors. Early afternoon was the best time for this. The chambermaids were almost finished with the rooms, and most of the guests had gone out for the day. If Dean tried earlier, the maid carts were still in the way, and later at night guests were either running back to change for dinner or complaining once it was time for them to sleep.

Over the past twelve days, he'd worked every shift on the schedule. The resort didn't need as many staff through the later part of the night/early morning, but there were still accidents or lights out or other problems in the guest rooms. He'd gotten a crash course in plumbing and electrical work and had been used as a delivery boy when someone forgot a toothbrush or shaving cream.

After finishing the third floor, he unplugged the vacuum and hauled it to the service elevator, then pressed the button for the fourth floor. Last one. As it rose, Dean twisted from side to side and arched his back. Ridiculous. He worked out daily at his home gym and was in great shape. Or so he thought until he came here. This job used some very different muscles from the ones he typically exercised.

The thing that bothered him most was being on his feet all day. It made his hip ache. All part of having one leg a half inch shorter than the other. He was too vain to use the lifts the doctor had recommended he get for one shoe. Plus, it never got rid of the limp anyway. Perhaps he had to bite the bullet and have his assistant send the one he had at the house.

How much longer would he be here, though? He had certainly gotten a clearer picture of how the resort ran. However, he wasn't any closer to figuring out who was sharing their marketing plans with the competition.

Aarya, he was pleased to see, was as efficient as they'd heard. No nonsense but pleasant, and she took care of problems as soon as they came up. Hugh, on the other hand, liked to wait until it was Aarya's shift to fix something. Or he put the onus on Eleni and had her do it. With what she was paid, it wasn't her responsibility to do management level tasks.

As it was, he'd noticed how busy she was after she'd been out for a day. When he'd popped into the office for trash or other cleaning, she'd been rushing around or typing away. Yet, she always managed a smile and kind word for him.

He'd have to chat with Trey and see why they didn't have two admin assistants for this location. They could cover the early day, late evening, weekday, and weekend shifts and not have so much catch up work the next day. Was that even a decision they made at corporate? Seemed like they gave the managers a budget and each had to work within it, depending on their financial output.

How many decisions did he make without knowing exactly what went on in the resorts? His brother visited them each a few times a year. Dean only looked at them on paper. Yes, he'd been to each one several times, but never officially. In person, the running of them was very different.

He wasn't deeply disturbed by what he saw here. For the most part, the place was run efficiently, and the staff worked hard. Very hard. But he'd noticed many of them stayed distant, like him, and were almost afraid of being caught taking a short break.

Just yesterday, he'd seen Hugh scold one of the chambermaids for using the restroom in between cleaning rooms. He also knew she'd been working her butt off all morning and had just finished a room that had been tossed by a group of rich party boys. He'd had to help her get the mattress back on the bed and wet vac the pizza and beer they'd spilled all over the carpet. He'd even assisted in cleaning up the bodily fluids they'd left in the bathroom. She'd been very appreciative but scurried off like a frightened mouse after Hugh lambasted her.

Never in his life had he wanted to toss off his Dean Peter's persona so quickly and declare who he really was. But then he'd fail to accomplish the task that had brought him here in the first place.

He finished up the guest areas on the fourth floor and peeked into the financial office here to see if it was a good time to clean. Eleni was inside chatting with the accounts payable clerk, her smile refreshing and addictive. Every time he'd seen her since he'd started, she'd been extremely friendly to him. He shouldn't feel special. She was that way with everyone. Yet he'd been seeing her in a different light since finding out she wasn't married.

Stupid really, because it wasn't like they'd be starting a relationship. He was here for one reason. Okay, two, since he'd now seen that experiencing the resort from the inside was beneficial. He wanted to spend more time here.

Moving to the end of the hall, he pulled out his phone and shot off a text to Maggie, his assistant, to send his shoe lift to his address here on Last Chance Beach. As he scrolled through a few more messages—there were so many with him not fully in his office—the door to the finance office opened, and Eleni strode out.

She smiled his way, then her eyes got big, and she darted over to him.

Shaking her head, she said, "You shouldn't be using your phone during working hours. It's a strict rule with management."

"Oh, yeah. Sorry." He slid the phone into his pocket and gave her a quasi-smile.

"I don't have a problem with it. Most of us work hard and occasionally need to check in with someone. But it's a rule that management follows to the letter. I wouldn't want to see you reprimanded or fired because of it."

No one else was in the hallway, and they were both out of eyesight of the people in the financial office. "Did Hugh or Aarya make that rule?"

"No, it's from corporate."

"Have you ever met the owners?" Was she one of the ladies his brother had bragged about? Doubtful she was the type, but why did even the thought of that make him angry?

Eleni laughed. "I met one of the brothers once. Demitrius, I think, but I didn't say any more to him than hi. He seemed busy with some of the other staff."

Most likely Reva. Or any one of the other sexy, available women who worked here. The front desk was stacked with them. According to employee files, most of them had been hired by Hugh.

"Well, thank you for having my back. I appreciate it. I won't do it again."

She inched closer and placed her hand on his arm. "If you really need to make or take a call, go inside the restroom. That way no one sees you. I know it's kind of gross to take the phone in the bathroom, but at least you won't get fired."

The warmth of her hand on his skin tingled. What a ridiculous word, and he was sure he'd never used it before, but it was the only word he could think of to describe the feeling of her touch.

"My kids know they can't call unless it's an emergency, and they have to use the hotel landline to my office." Her eyes rose, and she shrugged. "That is if I'm there. Guess I should get back to work. It was nice seeing you again. It's too bad we never have time to chat. But the resort is busy and that's a good thing."

Dean patted her hand as she released his arm and strode down the hall away from him. His phone vibrated in his pocket, and he took a second to step into the utilities closet next to the elevator before checking it. Just Maggie letting him know she'd send his lift overnight mail. Yeah, that wasn't an emergency.

He was the one who'd put that rule in place, but now that he'd lived it, it seemed a little overkill. Sure, he didn't want staff staring at their phones all day, but pulling it out to check a few times a day certainly wouldn't hurt. The staff he'd seen here so far were all great workers.

This phone rule just might interfere with his job of finding the marketing thief. And what about Eleni and her kids? What if they got hurt or needed something? Why shouldn't they be able to call her? Who was even watching them when she worked? Her partner in homeschooling? Someone else? They didn't seem old enough to stay on their own.

He shouldn't be worried about her, but she was a good employee. His father had always said to reward the good workers, because you want to keep them. Maybe he and Trey had allowed the managers to take over that responsibility, but *they* owned the company. The staff ultimately worked for them. Thoughts rushed through his head of changes he'd like to make. He should get them jotted down so he didn't forget.

But first, he had to vacuum the financial offices.

CHAPTER FOUR

*E*leni stacked the pile of paychecks on her desk and closed out of her computer. Even though most of the resort employees had direct deposit, there were still some holdovers who liked the paycheck in hand.

Grabbing the envelopes, she poked her head in to let Aarya know where she was going, then sauntered toward the reception area. She enjoyed this job every Friday. It got her out of the office and let her visit the staff and see what was happening in the resort.

As she strolled away from the administrative offices, Hugh popped out of the room behind the registration desk. She didn't even want to know what he was doing back there. The man had a reputation with the ladies.

When he saw her, he froze, then glared. "What are you doing out here? You aren't off shift for another half hour. You can't possibly have gotten all that work finished that I gave you."

The work he'd given her that he should have done. So often she felt like letting Aarya know how much Hugh put on her shoulders that he was supposed to be doing, but he'd obviously know it was her that tattled. Eleni couldn't afford to lose this job. There weren't many on the island that paid enough for her to live on with the kids and her mom, so she sucked it up and worked through lunch at times if she had to. Or brought some work home if she could.

Holding up the stack of envelopes, she waved them at him. "Paychecks. They need to be delivered before people clock out."

Hugh scowled and shook his head. "I don't know why they can't come to the office to get them."

"It would take them away from their jobs. I don't mind. It doesn't take long." With that, she smiled and stepped past him to the registration desk.

After a few minutes chatting with the front desk clerks, one of whom exited the back room tugging on her rumpled uniform, she moseyed to the kitchen area and peeked in on Chef and his crew. The smells always made her stomach growl.

Vlad caught her eye and beckoned her in. "Eleni, come give me your opinion on this new appetizer I created."

She laughed and crossed the room. Chef Vlad always had something for her to taste test, whether it was still under consideration or something that had been on the menu for years.

"Happy to help."

He handed her a napkin with a puff pastry on it. She stared at it suspiciously. There was nothing like this currently on the menu.

"What's in it? You know I'm allergic to nuts."

Vlad waved his hand. "No nuts. It's a shrimp, crabmeat blend with cream cheese and herbs."

"Ooh, that sounds yummy." She bit in, and her taste buds exploded. "Wow, that's incredible. Now, I wish I didn't have my paycheck already spent. I'd bring the kids here tonight just for these."

Vlad got a gleam in his eye and rushed over to the prep counter. He scooped up something and tucked it in a to-go bag. "I'll put this on the table right near the door. Make sure to take it before you leave tonight."

She pressed a kiss to Vlad's cheek. "You're too good to me. Thank you. I'm sure my mom and the kids will love them."

"Tell Georgina I made them just for her. Last we spoke, she mentioned something her grandmother used to make in Greece. I'm not sure these are exactly like them, but hopefully they will still be enjoyable."

Even though Vlad was eight years her mother's junior, he always spoiled the older woman if she had a chance to visit. Could he be sweet on her or was he simply being nice?

"I'll make sure to get them before I go. Thank you." She finished the last bite, wiped her hands on a nearby towel, then turned towards the conference rooms. There were eight smaller rooms that could be opened up in different configurations to make them into two or more larger rooms.

She handed paychecks to two waitstaff, who scurried over as soon as they saw her. Sometimes, she felt like she was feeding treats to puppies.

The only check she had left was Dean's. His schedule was so erratic, she wasn't sure where he'd be right now. In the past month, he'd been here almost every shift she had, but he'd also done many others. Basically, he'd been plunked in wherever they needed extra help. He still remained quiet and to himself, but she'd managed to get a smile from him a couple times. And boy, did it make a difference. He was a handsome man by any standard, but when he smiled and it reached his eyes, it was deadly.

His work ethic was second to none. He'd made it a point to learn about all aspects of the resort and even what the chain of command was and who was in charge of what, and not just his own department.

Wandering down the hallway, she peeked in the doorways of most of the rooms. There were some activities tonight, and the event staff was bustling around, setting up chairs and tables and placing cloths to cover them.

Her thoughts must have conjured him up, because Dean exited the restroom with a mop and rolling bucket. Before she could reach him with his paycheck, Reva waylaid him.

"Where are the extra rectangle tables I need from the Diamond Ballroom? I asked you for them fifteen minutes ago."

Sometimes, Eleni wanted to wrap duct tape around that woman's mouth. Poor Dean lowered his eyes and frowned.

"I thought clean bathrooms would be more important than tables for food that wouldn't come out for another two hours. Guests will be here long before that."

Reva shook her blonde mane. "You thought? You aren't paid to think here. That's my job. Your job is to do as I say."

Eleni hurried closer. Technically, Dean did what Santos told him to.

Reva planted her hands on her generous hips and looked about ready to fly off the handle.

"Reva, I'm sorry. I needed Dean for something, so it put him behind in his duties. That's on me. Don't you have event staff to haul tables back and forth from the rooms?"

The woman huffed but backed down. Even though Eleni wasn't a manager, she was in tight enough with them that Reva wouldn't want to rock the boat.

"There are three functions going on at the same time, and they all start in an hour. These rooms need to be set up and now. I needed the extra help."

"Of course, you do. I understand." Eleni softened her words. "My suggestion is to figure exactly how much staff you'll need for these things and plan accordingly. If you need more, you have to make sure to let Hugh know when he does scheduling."

Reva rolled her eyes and faked a smile.

"The bathrooms are on Dean's list. However, the tables are not, and the bathrooms are indeed more important than the tables getting in place a few hours early."

She faced Dean who'd stood by silently. He was good at that. "Is everything else finished on your list? I believe you were scheduled to leave a half hour ago."

"The bathroom was last. I'll get the tables before I punch out."

Eleni patted his arm. "Excellent. I'll help you get the tables. Reva, will that do?"

Reva faked her smile again and pivoted on her heels. "Yes, thank you."

As they ambled down the hall toward the largest ballroom, Eleni handed Dean his check. "You've earned this and then some, huh?"

"Thanks for stepping in back there," he said as he slipped the envelope in his back pocket.

She shrugged. "It's nothing."

He took a moment to deposit the rolling mop and bucket in a storage room, then joined her again. "May I ask you something, honestly?"

"Of course."

"Do you like Reva?"

That wasn't what she'd expected. Since she hated to badmouth anyone, and it was hardly professional of her to do so, she gave a half truth. "She does a fairly good job."

He chuckled. The sound was nice, and Eleni wanted to hear it again.

"Fairly good, huh? That's not exactly a glowing report."

Eleni sighed as they crossed the Diamond Ballroom to the back where the tables were stored. "All the activities she plans are directed at adults. I know the resort doesn't really cater much to children, but I think they should. Of course, maybe it's just because I have two kids. But they're missing out on a large market. There's so much you can do for families, and they come back if they've been treated well."

"Kids?" The face he made was comical.

Now, she laughed. "I know. I suppose kids would make your job even harder. Let's face it, they aren't exactly the neatest humans on this planet.

Dean glanced over his shoulder to where they'd just come from. "They might be messier, but many of them are nicer to be around."

The evening sky was gorgeous tonight, and Dean loved looking at it. His apartment wasn't anywhere near the water, but if he walked only a few streets over he could get there quick enough to catch the sunset. Tonight, though, he was walking in the other direction. Past Eleni's house.

He told himself it was only because the roads were flatter this way. It had nothing to do with wanting to see her. A couple of times, he'd gotten a glimpse of her standing at her kitchen window.

Her house was a cute one-story cottage on a corner lot only two streets over from his rental. There was a small yard with two sections of picket fencing that separated the corner from the street. A flower bed spread out behind the fencing, with local flora artfully arranged. He couldn't even begin to name what the plants were, nor did he care.

He'd changed out of his uniform and put on worn jeans and a t-shirt. The night was still warm. What a difference from early October back in New England. Not that Boston didn't have some warmer days, but once that sun went down, so did the temps.

Noise from the yard drifted over as he approached Eleni's house. Her kids were running around with a woman who had to be Eleni's mother. They shared the same dark hair, though this woman's had some gray sprinkled throughout. Maybe less than he did. The smile she beamed at the children was as warm and sweet as Eleni's.

He tried not to stare as he sauntered by. Lots of people walked around the island or rode bikes, so seeing someone out for a nightly stroll was common. Even so, today he was walking on her side of the road.

"Dessert." Eleni called out, the word causing Dean to freeze for a second. He lowered his head and shuffled past, not wanting to be caught stalking her.

"Dean? Hello. How are you?"

Popping his head up, he added a surprised expression and a head nod. "Hey. You live here?"

The kids came running over, and Xander hopped up and down in front of him. "Hi, Mr. Dean. Remember me? I'm Xander. I asked if you wanted to play basketball, remember?"

It was hard to ignore the exuberance of the boy. "I remember you. And your sister. Thea, right?"

"Yes. It's Anthea, but my nickname is Thea. You can call me that, too."

"Thank you, Thea. You can call me Dean. I'm not a super formal guy."

Xander ducked his head. "Mom makes us call all the old people Mr. and Mrs. and their name. Says it's out of respect."

Dean wasn't sure if he should be insulted at the old people comment, but he supposed compared to these kids, he certainly was.

Dean glanced at Eleni and grinned. "It's a good thing for her to teach you manners. That's an important skill to have in life."

"I just brought brownies out for the kids. Would you like one, Dean?" She held out a plate with scrumptious chocolate decadence on it. They smelled incredible. When was the last time he'd eaten a homemade brownie?

"I, um, don't want to intrude. I was just taking a walk after dinner."

"What did you eat?" Xander asked, chomping a large bite from the dessert. "We had pork chops and rice pilaf."

"That sounds nice. I, um, just had some macaroni."

Thea raised her eyes to him. "Did it have sauce and cheese with bread crumbs sprinkled over the top and was it baked in the oven? That's how Mom makes it. It's really good."

"No, it was plain. Well, I added a little butter to it." He didn't have a whole lot of food in his apartment. After a month here, you'd think he'd get used to the fact dinner wasn't waiting for him in the kitchen like back home.

Thea made a face. "You need to get Mom to give you her recipe. Way better than plain with butter." Thea grabbed her brownie, then sauntered off to sit on a chair near the older woman.

"If you've got time, come on over and meet my mom." Eleni cocked her head toward the table and chairs that were near the house.

"Mom, this is Dean. I work with him." Eleni did something with her hands when she introduced him. Sign Language?

"It's nice to meet you, Dean. Eleni mentioned you just moved here. Have you enjoyed the island so far?"

Her voice was clear, and Dean got confused. Was the woman deaf or had he misunderstood what Eleni had done before.

"My mom lost her hearing over the past three years. We've been dabbling in American Sign Language, so she can understand us better. But her speech is still fine. Just face her when you talk and speak slow, but not so your lips do weird things."

"It's nice to meet you, too. I like the island." He kept it plain and simple. Hopefully, she got the message. He eyed Eleni. "How do I say that in sign language?"

Eleni swept one hand over the other, then touched her fists together with her index fingers raised. Then, she pointed to her mother. He repeated the gestures. Her mom beamed.

"He's a fast learner, and so sweet to accommodate me. I'm Georgina Matsoukas. You can call me Georgie. Have a seat and a brownie."

Eleni had set the plate on the table and lowered herself to one of the chairs. He settled in between her and Thea and reached for a brownie.

Xander finished the chocolate confection, then grabbed a basketball by his feet. "Mom, I'm going to shoot some hoops, okay? Can you come, Mr. Dean?"

"Let him eat his brownie first. And watch for cars," Eleni warned.

"I'll go play with him. I can still throw a ball in the net." Georgina got up, followed by Thea, and tagged along behind Xander. Dean grinned when the older woman stole the ball from her grandson and swished it right through the hoop.

"Matsoukas?" He glanced at Eleni "You're Greek? But Griffin...?"

Eleni shook her head. "My husband wasn't Greek. Mom lived in Greece until she was about ten. I grew up in the States."

"Your husband? I never asked—"

"He passed away five years ago."

Something Dean already knew, but he could hardly explain how he knew.

"I'm sorry. The children must have been very young."

Her gaze strayed to where they played on the quiet street. Most of the streets on the island were quiet. Unless you were going from one side of the island to the other, many locals walked, took bikes, or the occasional golf cart.

"Yes, they were three. Unfortunately, they don't remember him much." Frowning, she looked at her feet.

"Greece. Have you ever been there?" Better to change the subject.

A smile danced across her face. That was more like it. Her eyes turned dreamy, and she sighed. "No, but I'd love to go and bring Mom back there. Show the kids where she grew up. A little piece of their past."

Suddenly, he wanted to give her that. Just to see her smile like she was.

"Yios has a resort on Mykonos, you know."

Her laugh split the air. "Yes, but can you imagine what airfare for four people would be? Plus, I doubt I'd get free hotel rooms." She patted his arm. "It's not really in my budget at the moment. Maybe someday."

Someday? Like when she'd sold a few more marketing ideas? He hated the thought of her resorting to that. When she got up and began playing basketball with her kids, he had a hard time seeing her in the role of spy.

He finished his brownie, then joined them in throwing the ball around. Both Georgina and Eleni were better than him. Luckily, he could still out throw the kids. Like that was an accomplishment to be proud of.

Strangely, he enjoyed dribbling the ball and passing it to the others, while they all ribbed each other, but also cheered each other on when someone was shooting the ball. When the sun had sunk far below the horizon and there were only shadows left dancing on the street, they headed back to the table and all grabbed another brownie.

"Thanks for sharing dessert with me. I haven't had a homemade brownie in a long time. These are delicious."

"Will you come back and play basketball with us again?" Xander asked between bites. Thea jumped up and down, nodding her head.

"I might have to in order to get some practice. I can't have your mother and grandmother beating me, can I? That wouldn't look too cool."

"You can practice here anytime. The neighbors are only here in the summer, but they let us use their hoop all year long."

"That's very nice of them." He'd noticed most of the islanders were extremely friendly and helpful. The woman who rented him the apartment had checked on him once a week to make sure everything was running okay. It was an old building that needed some work, but it was clean and well kept.

"I guess I should be going. I've got to work tomorrow." He faced Eleni. "You're in, too, right?"

She glanced at her watch. "Yes, and seven AM comes very early. It was nice to see you out and about, Dean. You'll have to stop by more often. The kids enjoyed it."

As he walked away, he realized he'd enjoyed it as well. The night hadn't been like any other he'd ever experienced, and that wasn't a bad thing. He'd been living in his own little world for so long he'd forgotten what the rest of it felt like.

Guilt ate him up as he devoured the last bite of brownie. He wasn't being honest with Eleni, and he hated lying to her and her family. They seemed like decent people. He doubted she was involved in hurting the resort. But he'd been wrong before.

CHAPTER FIVE

*T*welve-thirty was the perfect time for lunch on Fridays. Eleni had gotten through all of her morning correspondence, and the weekend visitors hadn't checked in yet. Not that she had much to do with check-in, but she had to make sure Aarya or Hugh was available to deal with any guests that needed special attention. When that happened, Eleni was the one the front desk called.

As she glanced out the window, Dean walked through the garden patio, having just hung up some lights for an event tonight. Again, not his job. Most likely, either Reva or Chuck, the events coordinator, had grabbed him and put him to work. The man never said no even when he had his own work to do, and often he went without lunch to get the extra tasks done.

Not today. Eleni wouldn't let him. Peeking her head into Aarya's office, she asked, "Is there anything else you need me to do immediately, boss? I finished those two e-mails you needed to go out and gathered the numbers for next week's registrations. They should be in your inbox."

Aarya looked up from her computer screen and smiled. "Excellent, Eleni. Thank you. No, nothing pressing at this moment. Is everything okay?"

"Fine. I just figured I'd take lunch if there wasn't anything you needed right now."

Waving her hand, Aarya shook her head. "You know I trust you to take your breaks when it's convenient. How are the kids? Is school going well this year?"

"They're fine and so is my mom. School is great, though I'd be thrilled if the town finally got moving on that elementary school they've been talking about for years."

Aarya rolled her eyes. She was on several town committees and knew the amount of red tape that could mess up the simplest of plans.

"Let me know if you need any time off to help Xander or Thea with something. You do more in the time you're here than most people could do in a double shift. Don't think I don't appreciate that."

The warmth of knowing she'd done a good job flowed through her. "Thanks. I'll be back in a half hour."

"Don't rush back. It's gorgeous outside today. The work will wait. Maybe I'll give some of it to Hugh to do tonight." She chuckled, then lowered her head back to her own work.

Eleni scooped up her lunch bag and trotted through the Breakfast Room to the outside door. He was still there.

"Dean, do you have a minute?" she called out as he checked off something on a clipboard.

When he tipped his head up and saw her, his face lit up with that devastating smile of his. God, it practically knocked her off her feet.

He opened the small storage shed next to the building and hung the clipboard on a hook. After closing and locking it, he wandered her way.

"Hi, Eleni. Did you need something?"

"You need something. Lunch. You haven't taken it yet."

Peeking at his watch, he frowned. "I'll have to take it later. I've got too much to do right now."

She shook her head, and the soft ocean breeze caught a few strands of her hair and blew them away from her neck. "You won't take it later. You always vacuum the guest floors at one, then do another round of trash, followed by cleaning up the grounds and the beach area. That is if you don't get pulled into doing something else."

His lips twisted to the side, and he half rolled his eyes. "You know how this place runs."

"I do. I also know you don't get paid for a half hour each day, regardless of whether you take a lunch or not. So I need to make sure you take it. Follow me."

She pivoted on her heel and stalked away, hoping he'd do what she asked. As she entered the hotel and strode to the room behind registration, she heard his soft, uneven steps behind her.

She picked up the two-way radio that sat in the charging port and said, "I'll be down by the dock if anyone is looking for me. But only if it's an absolute emergency. Understand."

The clerk nodded. Eleni took Dean by the elbow and cocked her head toward the side exit. Once outside, she turned left, started down the walkway to the beach, then veered toward the dock.

She sat at one of the picnic tables and pointed to the bench next to her. "Have a seat."

His brows drew together, but he planted his bottom on the bench. "Thanks. I don't have a lunch, though."

Unzipping her bag, she began pulling out items. "I know. I brought you lunch. It's not much, but it's more than you typically eat."

"How do you know what I typically eat?"

She laughed. "It's my job to know everything that goes on here. That's what a good administrative assistant does. You usually grab some crackers or a granola bar and eat it while you're sweeping the tennis court."

A tiny smile crossed his face. "You are good. But I don't want to eat all your lunch."

Eleni pushed a plastic container towards him, then set one in front of her. "I brought enough for you and me. Now, eat. We've only got a half hour."

She handed him a fork. He dug into the pasta salad, then picked up the ham and cheese roll up. When he'd taken a few bites, he shifted so he faced her.

"You mentioned the resort should do more for kids and families. What kind of stuff would you implement?"

After wiping her mouth with a napkin, she cocked her head. "Why? Are you planning to take over and run the company someday?"

A strange expression crossed his face. "Maybe."

"Well, when you do, I'd like a chair with better lumbar support, please."

He scribbled on his hand like he was taking notes. "That's all? Nothing else?"

Eleni took a few more bites while thinking about his question. He finished his roll up, then worked on the pasta.

"Well, sure. I'd like to work fewer hours and get home to see my kids earlier, yet still have the same pay and better medical insurance."

"You don't have medical insurance?"

He was a full-time employee so must know what the benefits package was. Unless he thought because she worked in the admin office, she got something better.

"I do, but it's limited."

"What doesn't it cover that you need?"

Was this simply conversation or was he going somewhere with his questioning?

"I have a peanut allergy and need an EpiPen. They're super expensive, and our insurance doesn't cover prescriptions."

His eyes narrowed. "A nut allergy? Those are serious. You can die if you aren't treated right away. Is there a hospital on the island? Do you have an EpiPen now?"

"Not here. It's in my purse. I can't afford more than one." She gave a tiny laugh. "Although the one I have probably expired a few years ago."

"Wait, you don't have a current one?" Concern covered his face.

She shrugged. "It probably still works. Hopefully, I'll never need it. I'm very careful about what I eat and always ask about nuts whenever I have anything someone else prepared."

He gazed down at the now empty dish in front of him. "So that's why we've got ham instead of peanut butter and jelly."

"Yeah. I feel bad I can't make it for the kids, but I don't even keep it in the house. They'll get it at Nadine's sometimes, and she's diligent about making them wash their hands and face, and she checks they didn't get any on their clothes."

Those dark eyes bore into hers. "Why?"

"My allergy is pretty severe. Just the peanut oil can make me have a reaction."

"I wish I'd known. You need to make everyone at the resort aware of this." Dean cleaned up his plate and deposited it back in her bag.

"You don't have to avoid it just because of me."

He swung around on the bench to face her. "There're peanut butter crackers in the vending machine, and I get them often."

She nodded. "I know. Which is why I'm bringing you lunch."

His jaw tightened, and he took a deep breath in. "But if I get peanut butter on my hands, then touch stuff in your office, you could die." The expression on his face showed horror.

Placing her hand on his arm, she smiled at him. "You're constantly washing your hands, Dean. I've seen you. I'm sure I'll be fine."

"I won't be fine if you have an allergic reaction."

He placed his hand on top of hers. The feel of his skin touching hers was pleasant and made her so aware of him.

As he squeezed her hand, he said, "I'll make extra sure to wipe down any surfaces if I eat those crackers. Or maybe I won't get them anymore. I'd hate for something to happen to you."

"That's really sweet, Dean. I appreciate the concern. And that you spent your lunch break with me."

He chuckled. "Did I have a choice?"

"No." She stood and made sure to clean up everything they'd brought down. "You won't tomorrow either. I'm making chili tonight. With corn bread. I always make too much, so I'll need help getting rid of the leftovers. Are you up for that?"

"Do you make it hot?"

"Oh, yeah. Believe it or not, the kids like it that way."

As they strolled up the path toward the main resort, he mumbled, "I like it hot, too."

As Dean locked his door and headed down the stairs, his phone vibrated in his pocket. He peeked at the number. Trey. It had been a few weeks since he'd talked to his brother. Right now, he was on his way for a walk past Eleni's house. Who was he kidding? He'd been stopping by her place at least three or four times a week after dinner.

She'd invited him to join them a few times, but he felt guilty enough that he'd been eating her lunches every day and mooching dessert many nights, that he didn't feel right taking food from her at dinner as well. Especially since he knew what her salary was and that his was a bazillion times more. He couldn't even offer to give her money. She knew what Dean Peters' salary was, and it was barely enough to live on in his tiny apartment.

The phone stopped vibrating, then it pinged. Trey had sent a text. Best see what he wanted.

—*Have you stumbled on our mystery spy yet?*—

His fingers flew over the screen. —*Not yet.*—

—*You've been on the island for six weeks. I didn't think you would last six days away from your office. Have you suddenly found a long held desire to empty trash?*—

Dean chuckled. He hadn't thought he'd last this long either.

—*I'm taking the time to get to know the staff from a different perspective.*—

That was the truth. It was amazing what people said to you when they thought you were merely a maintenance worker. Things they'd be mortified to say to the owner of the resort.

—*Any potential suspects?*—

—*I'm narrowing it down. Not everyone has access to the information.*—

Of course, he'd discovered that people he'd thought wouldn't have access just might. Hugh had a habit of being overly friendly with some of the front desk clerks, the pool staff, and some waitresses. It was possible there were bedtime stories being told.

Aarya and Hugh were at the top of the list since they were in charge. However, they made enough of a salary that they wouldn't need more money. Who was he kidding? For some people, there was never enough money.

Reva and Chet also made a good salary, and in their positions of Activities Director and Events Coordinator, they'd have access to the marketing to accommodate the guests.

Lucy, the staff accountant, and Harry, the office manager, would need access to any budgets the marketing department came up with. Then, marketing itself, Glenn and Judy, would know all about the themes and ideas since they were the ones to come up with them. But why would they sell their ideas to another resort? Wouldn't it be simpler to just go work there?

Dean didn't have a clue what anyone's motivation would be to steal and sell their promotion. Except money. Without being able to access anyone's bank accounts, he couldn't tell who had extra cash coming in.

—*When do you think you'll be done?*

That was a good question. As he got closer to Eleni's house, he wasn't sure what his answer should be.

—*I've decided to stay a little longer. I want to do an in-depth assessment of staff and management. Lots of changes coming, but not until I get more information.*—

—*Have at it. The company's still standing without you at the helm.*—

Did his brother think he'd taken a vacation from his leadership position?

—*I'm working from here and delegating responsibilities to the heads of each department at corporate. I haven't deserted Yios. I just have a few different goals at the moment.*—

—*I hope one of them is enjoying what the island has to offer. Sun, sand, and sweet ladies.*—

There was certainly one sweet lady he'd been enjoying, though not in the way Trey meant. He loved the fact she, her mom, and her kids seemed to like him even without knowing how much he was worth. That was a first.

As was how much he liked spending time with them. He'd gotten better at playing basketball and could stay even with Georgie and Eleni now.

—I'd like to remain a bit longer to really inspect the inner workings of The Ocean Pearl. It's doing well, but I have a feeling there are ways we can turn an even bigger profit.—

—Have at it, bro. All's good at corporate. Just goes to show you don't need to work every hour of every day. Take time for yourself.—

—Great. I've got work to do right now. I'll keep in touch.—

He was almost at Eleni's.

Luckily, Trey took his hint and responded with a thumb's up emoji. Dean shut the ringer off and slipped the device in the pocket of his jeans.

"Mr. Dean, Mr. Dean, check this out," Xander called as he came into view. The boy dribbled the ball, then passed it behind his back and continued dribbling with the other hand.

"Excellent. You're getting really good at that."

"I'll show you how to do it and then you can get really good, too."

Dean chuckled as the boy gave him detailed instructions, then made him practice in slow motion. It took a few tries, but he managed to do it. "You're a great teacher. Maybe you should become a coach when you grow up."

Xander made a face. "I'm going to play professional basketball first. Then, when I get old, I can become a coach."

"Old like me?" Dean questioned, grinning.

Xander cocked his head and squinted. "Maybe even before that."

"Xander Griffin! I can't believe you just said that." Eleni stood with her hands planted on her hips at the bottom of the stairs.

"It's okay, Eleni. He's right that I'm a little too...mature...to be playing professional ball."

She crossed her arms over her chest and glared at her son. Xander had the grace to blush.

"I'm sorry, Mr. Dean. You aren't old. I shouldn't have said that."

"Thanks. But you're right that maybe professional basketball shouldn't be my goal right now."

Eleni called them over as she placed a pie on the table. Georgie came up behind carrying plates and forks. She handed one of each to Dean.

He thanked her in sign language, and she beamed. He still didn't know much, but he'd made it a point to learn a few new words each night he'd stopped by. Georgie confessed she was still learning, too. They could learn together.

Thea was first to devour her piece of apple pie, so she pulled out a stuffed dog and fiddled with a red bow on the animal's head.

"Cuddles looks exceptionally beautiful tonight. Is there a special reason?" Cuddles joined them most nights at dessert, and Dean discovered Thea liked talking about the toy.

The little girl threw him a huge smile. Like mother like daughter. "She knew you were coming over and wanted to look pretty. I wish she was a real dog."

Eleni laughed. "Right. Just what I need is one more mouth to feed and the extra duty of taking it for a walk every day."

"I'd do it. I'd walk my dog if it was real."

"That's nice, sweetie, but you aren't old enough to go for a walk by yourself."

She had a point. The islanders all looked out for each other, but with so many tourists coming and going, you could never be too careful.

"How old do I need to be to walk the dog by myself?"

"Older than you are now. But I sure could use to walk off that pie. I'm stuffed. Anyone want to go with me?"

Eleni stood and started cleaning up the dishes. Dean helped and brought them inside and filled her sink with soap and hot water. He'd been inside a few times, though never past the living room or kitchen. The house was small yet tidy and felt like home.

"Let them soak. Did you want to come for a walk with us? We'll go slow."

He tipped his head. "Because I'm so old?"

She bent over laughing, then held onto his arm. "No, so we can enjoy the beautiful night. I'm not much younger than you, and my mother is definitely older."

He patted her hand and stepped closer. "I think Georgina is younger than all of us."

She took a deep breath and focused her dark eyes on him. "You could be right."

She didn't move, and he wasn't sure he was able to either. This woman mesmerized him in ways he didn't understand. Lifting his hand, he touched her cheek, feeling the softness of her skin.

"Mom, are you coming?" Xander yelled from the front door.

Eleni shook her head like she'd just woken up. He knew exactly how she felt.

"I'd love to take a walk, if you don't mind keeping the speed down for the old guy." Mostly, he wanted more time with Eleni. Georgie and the kids were a bonus.

He held his arm out formally and said, "Madame, your escort awaits."

She curled her hand around his elbow and did a slight curtsy. "Thank you, kind sir."

As they strolled out and to the sidewalk to catch up to the kids, he knew kindness had nothing to do with it.

CHAPTER SIX

*O*nce they hit the sidewalk, Eleni released Dean's arm. Touching him like that got her heart racing, and she'd be out of breath in no time if she continued to hold his arm.

"The pie was delicious, Eleni. I won't fit in my uniform much longer if I continue to have dessert with you."

Slowing down so he could catch up, she gazed at his handsome face. "I've seen how hard you work around The Pearl. I don't think you need to worry." Every ounce of the man was perfection. She shouldn't even admit how often she simply watched him do his job. Her office had a great view of the garden patio, and she always seemed to need something in the filing cabinet near the window whenever he was working out there. Especially when he was on a stepladder hanging something. His shoulders bunched so nicely, and she couldn't help but stare.

"Hmm. So does that mean I could get another piece of pie at some point?" His mischievous expression made her stomach flip. He'd come out of his shell so much from those first weeks at the resort. It was lovely to see. He still remained distant from many at work, but around her and her family, he seemed to come alive.

"I might be persuaded to bring some in my lunch box tomorrow at work."

He shoved his hands into his back pockets, which only showcased his well developed chest. "What kind of persuasion are we talking about? Is it going to cost me much?"

What would he do if she said the payment was a kiss? Of course, she'd never been that bold in her life. She wasn't about to start now.

"We might be able to make a deal."

They walked in a comfortable silence for a few minutes, the kids chattering together up ahead.

"I hope the kids aren't too rambunctious for you. Do you have lots of family?" Okay, maybe that wasn't the most discreet of inquiries, but she'd been dying to know more about this man.

"Not much. My mom died when I was a teen and my father about ten years ago. I have one younger brother. I haven't seen him in a while, though we talk or text often enough. He's a bit of a playboy and isn't married or have any kids."

"Have you ever been married? Had kids?" He could be married now, but she highly doubted he'd visit every night if there was a wife at home.

His face tensed, and she regretted her question immediately. She grabbed his arm and squeezed. "I'm sorry. I shouldn't have asked. Forget it."

He placed his hand on hers and returned the pressure. "No, it's fine. I've never been married or had any kids. I had an accident when I was younger and can't have them."

How terrible. Eleni couldn't imagine not having her children. They were her life.

"I'm sorry. I didn't know. Is that why you come over?" She'd been hoping it might be her.

His eyes strayed up ahead to where her mother held the twins' hands as they skipped along.

"No, I usually try and avoid children if I can. But yours..."

She snorted. "Are so adorable you can't help yourself, right?"

He paused in his step and stared down at her. "Actually, they are. So is their mother." His gaze swung away, and Eleni could have sworn his face got redder. "And their grandmother," he added quickly.

A shiver ran down her spine with his admission, but she wasn't ready for any kind of personal discussion, not with her kids so close.

"So, it's not just my baking skills," she teased.

A grin popped up as he cocked his head. "Well, that, too."

His thumb ran back and forth over the skin on her hand, and she became aware she hadn't let go of his arm yet. But she didn't want to.

Thea darted back to where she and Dean were, breathless. "Mom, we're gonna run back to the house. Me and Xander need to get our supplies ready for when Miss Nadine takes us tomorrow. Yia Yia said take your time, and if you go by the market, to stop and get more bread. There isn't much left."

"Okay, be good for your grandmother. I'll be back in a bit."

As the kids ran off, with her mom skipping behind them, Eleni faced Dean. "The corner market is a few streets over, near the marina. If you want to head back—"

"I'll go with you. It's a nice night for a walk. I'm not used to it being this balmy in mid-October. New England tends to chill up real fast once the sun goes down."

"If you're sure you don't mind, I'd love the company. I sit at my desk all day, so it feels good to get up and move. Oh, and thank you for the chair with the lumbar support. Where did you get that?"

Dean shrugged. "It was in one of the back storage rooms. I remembered you said that was your dearest wish."

"Does this mean you're my fairy godmother now?"

"Your wish is my command."

She hugged his arm tighter. "Ooh, I'll have to come up with a really good wish for the next one. If I'd known it would come true, I wouldn't have wasted it on a chair."

As they got closer to the shore, the sound of waves carried to them, and she sighed.

"You okay?" He peered down at her.

"Mmhmm. I love the ocean and all that goes with it."

"Guess that's why you live on an island."

They arrived at the market, and Dean held the door open for her. As she picked out a loaf of bread that was far more than she wanted to pay, Dean wandered down the aisle.

When she'd finished her purchase, she found him staring at the cases of beer. Clenching her jaw, she asked, "Did you need something?"

His head snapped up, and he narrowed his eyes. Had she sounded that bad?

"No, I'm ready to go." He held the door open for her again, and they exited the store. When they got to the path that led to the shore, she stopped as a shiver overtook her.

Dean stepped closer and touched her shoulder. "Are you all right? You seem a little off."

Did she tell him what was bothering her? He'd shared about his inability to have kids earlier. Perhaps a bit of her background was in order.

"That path down there is where my husband died."

"What? I never asked what happened?"

Holding the bread in one hand, she linked her other arm with his elbow and began walking.

"My husband, Sean, was a very good man. Kind to everyone and always ready to help if someone needed it. But he was an alcoholic. He never drank while at work or if he was driving, but he drank. Every single day. A lot."

Dean's gaze heated her skin, even in the cooler evening air. "Did he ever hurt you or the kids?"

"No, he wasn't a violent or angry drunk. Just a stupid drunk. He sat at home, watching or listening to sports, and he drank. Usually until he passed out. Or fell on the floor, which sometimes woke him up. Sometimes, it didn't. He typically didn't start until I put the kids to bed, fortunately. Often, I went to bed, too, so I didn't have to watch him as he got more and more pathetic."

"I'm sorry, Eleni. He died from an accident?"

Taking a deep breath, she continued. Maybe it was time to vent a little. She'd never wanted anyone who knew him to think poorly of him, so she'd kept it all in.

"I begged him, a lot, to stop drinking. Or at least not to drink quite so much. It worked for a day or two, but then he'd sit down and hammer them back. He couldn't stop. Once he had a sip, he kept going. I threatened to leave him if he didn't slow down. He promised me he would. And for a while, he didn't bring any alcohol into the house."

Their steps were slow as they traversed the streets back to her house. Dean held her arm close to his body but let her talk.

"After a while, I realized he was still drinking. He was an electrician and often had jobs off-island. He'd call and tell me he was running late on a job. Then, later, once I was in bed, he'd stumble in reeking of alcohol."

"He was driving while drunk?" Dean's tone was low and rough.

"No, he'd go to the bar at the marina, park there, then walk home. But one day, he was so plastered, he staggered out of the bar and wandered too close to the shore. He stumbled, hit his head on a rock, and fell in the water. He drowned." She had to stop before the tears welling in her eyes spilled over. She hadn't cried for Sean Griffin in years.

Dean slipped his hand out of hers and wrapped it around her shoulder. God, that felt good. How long had it been since a man gave her comfort like this? Probably since before Sean died.

"I'm so sorry, Eleni. You didn't deserve that."

"No. The kids didn't either. And because he couldn't control his drinking, they get to grow up without a father and lots of other things, because I sure can't bring in the kind of money he did. If it weren't for my mother and her pension, doubtful we could stay on the island."

"He didn't have any kind of savings or insurance policy?" Dean sounded like he was almost growling.

"There was a small insurance policy that paid for his funeral, and I managed to pay off half the mortgage, which made my monthly payment smaller. But it's tough to make ends meet. I don't need to tell you about struggling financially. It's tough on everyone, especially when the island gets quiet in the winter. Not as many tourists."

Dean hugged her tighter against him and pressed his lips to her hair. Could she tip her head up and demand one for her lips?

"I'm so sorry," Dean said again. "If there's anything I can do..."

"Thank you. That's sweet. But it was five years ago. We've managed until now, and we'll manage in the future."

"I'm sure it still hurts."

"I can forgive him for drinking, and I can forgive him for dying. But the one thing I hate more than anything is that he lied to me. He told me he'd stop. Then, he didn't, but he pretended he did. It's the one thing he had control over."

Dean's arm slipped off her shoulder, and she wanted to cry. But soon he took her hand in his as they strolled. The remainder of the journey was quiet, but he held her hand the entire way.

❧

Entering the administration offices, the first thing Dean saw was Eleni bent over to reach inside a filing cabinet. She swiveled at the sound of the door, and a huge smile grew on her face. The one he'd gotten used to seeing almost every day. If one of them wasn't working, he'd make it a point to take his evening stroll past her house. One of the family always invited him to have dessert with them.

"Hi, Dean. How are you today?" She shuffled papers in her hands, then settled in her chair again. Even though she always inquired how people were, Eleni wasn't the type to stop her work while she chatted. Did they have other employees at other locations who were as dedicated as she was? How could they find out? Something like this should be rewarded.

"There was a huge mess in one of the rooms this morning, so I had to give Maria a hand cleaning it up."

She narrowed her eyes. "Did you give up your lunch break to catch up on your work?"

He shrugged. "Vlad gave me a few samples when I mopped the prep kitchen floor after the lunch crowd."

"Something good, I hope."

"From Vlad, it's always good. I need to do trash. They in?"

"Hugh is in his office. Aarya is in a meeting with a vendor in the conference room."

Dean gave a curt nod and quickly emptied the trash in the manager's office. He was hoping Hugh would finish what he was working on and leave before he had to do that room.

No luck. The man was still there. But then he fiddled with some papers on his desk and stood as Dean opened the door.

Hugh shook something off the papers, then waved at the desk. "Clean that mess off my desk while you're at it." No please or thank you from the assistant manager. Ever.

When he moved closer, he saw the mess was a pile of peanut shells. Whipping his head around, Dean froze. Was he giving those papers to Eleni?

Panic hit him, and he dashed from the office just as Hugh was handing the files to Eleni. Grabbing them quickly, he sighed. She hadn't actually touched them.

Two sets of eyes stared at him like he was crazy.

"What in the world are you doing? Are you looking for a reason for me to fire you?" Hugh sputtered and attempted to rip the papers from his hands. Dean pulled them away.

"He's been eating peanuts," Dean said to Eleni, and her eyes widened. Was she frightened of the peanuts or because Hugh threatened to fire him?

"Thank you." A timid smile flashed his way again.

Hugh cleared his throat, his expression livid. "What is going on?"

Eleni's soft voice calmly said, "I have a peanut allergy. Even touching the oil can make me have a reaction. Dean was just being cautious."

"How was I supposed to know this?" Hugh's face turned red.

Eleni bit her lip, then said, "I've mentioned it a few times."

Hugh's head shook back and forth like he was trying to get water out of his ears. "I can't remember everyone's medical history. We've got over a hundred employees at this resort."

Dean stepped closer to the desk. "Eleni works with you, right here in the same office. I'd think for her safety, you'd remember something as important as this."

Hugh's death glare would have disintegrated him if he didn't own the entire resort. Dean carefully placed the papers on the table across from Eleni's desk. "Don't touch those. I'll help you with them in a minute."

Grabbing his spray bottle and a roll of paper towels from his cart, Dean went back into Hugh's office, cleaned up the shells, then wiped down anything Eleni might have access to. He did the same thing in the outer office, making sure to get door handles and the knobs on the copier and coffee machine.

Once he'd tied the trash bag closed, Dean cocked his head at Hugh, who stood by the window staring at the pool. "I suggest you wash your hands with lots of soap to get any oil off before you touch anything."

Focusing on Eleni again, he said, "I can help with whatever that is you need to type. I'll read it off to you while you put it in the computer."

Hugh whirled at this and spit flew from his mouth. "That's hotel business and isn't for any old eyes to see. Certainly not someone in the maintenance department."

Dean held up the papers and thrust them at Hugh. "Then, here. You can read them to her."

"I hardly have time to do that. This is her job, and if she can't do it, then we can find someone who can. As for you, I can always find a new maintenance worker. Dime a dozen."

Dean was tempted to say that was about all he made, then realized the company he ran set some of the pay rates. It would be one of the first things he'd fix once he was back being Konstantine Petrakis again.

Maybe even before, once he managed a meeting with his financial officer brother.

Eleni stood, her expression anxious. She couldn't afford to lose her job, but he'd never let that happen. Even if it meant not figuring out who the marketing thief culprit was, he'd make sure Eleni was fine.

"You'll do nothing of the sort, Hugh." Aarya stood in the open doorway, her arms crossed. How long had she been standing there?

Hugh's finger jabbed in Dean's direction. "I will not tolerate disrespect from an employee."

"I didn't see any disrespect. Not from Dean. Seems to me he was merely protecting Eleni. The last thing we'd ever want to do is harm any of the staff or guests, however accidentally."

Hugh's eyes blazed, but he bit his tongue. It was the first smart thing he'd done all day. Dean had to bite his own with the reprimands and threats he had swirling around in his mind.

Aarya clicked across the room and took the papers. "I'll give you a hand with these since you can't safely touch them. Unless you want to redo them after washing your hands, Hugh?"

He looked down his nose at all of them, then huffed out of the office. Dean gathered his cleaning supplies and the bag of trash and cocked his head at the ladies. "Do you need me to do anything else in here?"

Aarya smiled at him. "No, thank you, Dean. I appreciate your quick thinking and actions with the peanuts. I would be horrified if my best employee got sick. I wouldn't be able to run this place without her."

Eleni's cheeks turned pink, and she lowered her gaze to her computer.

"Just in the right place at the right time with the right knowledge. I wouldn't want anything to happen to your best employee either. Have a nice day."

Eleni's grateful gaze followed him as he wheeled his cart down the hallway to the storage closet. After rolling it inside, he stepped in after and closed the door.

Digging his phone from his pocket, he thought about Eleni and what would have happened if she'd touched those papers. A shiver ran through him. He thumbed his phone on, then sent a text to his brother with a copy to his admin assistant. He needed to find Eleni a new EpiPen, and he needed it fast.

CHAPTER SEVEN

*E*leni stifled a grin as she passed by her mother's room. Mom stood in front of the mirror, dragging a lipstick tube across her mouth. Vlad was stopping by this afternoon to try out some new recipes and to ask her mom how to improve them. Most likely, he just wanted to spend some time with her. They both insisted they were only friends, and she'd never seen them do anything that was more than friendly, but it would be lovely if her mom could find some companionship beyond that of her daughter and grandchildren.

Entering the living room, Eleni waved at the twins. "Can you tidy up some of these toys, so the house doesn't look like a bomb went off? It would be nice for visitors to not have to watch their step as they attempt to maneuver through this minefield."

Xander grabbed a handful of Legos and tossed them in a plastic tub. "Is Mr. Dean coming over? Can he play basketball with us?"

"I think Mr. Dean might be working today." Who was she kidding? She knew his schedule by heart. He got out at three today since he'd gone in early to set up for a wedding event.

Xander's entire frame slumped, and his head hung down. So dramatic, but she kind of felt the same. Dean had been taking his nightly strolls past their house often lately. She hoped maybe it wasn't random.

"If Yia Yia doesn't need us once Chef Vlad is here, we could possibly go for a walk downtown or to the beach." The traffic on a Sunday afternoon, even in October, would be heavier, but if they took side roads, they could avoid much of it.

Thea bounced over, Cuddles held tightly to her chest. "We could walk past Mr. Dean's house and see if he's home. I mean later, if we go for a walk. He might want to go downtown or to the beach, also."

Her sneaky children. She couldn't blame them. Dean had a charisma to him that made everyone like him. Those that got to know him, that is.

Except maybe Hugh. Eleni remembered the scene yesterday with the peanuts on Hugh's desk. Thank God Dean had noticed. She didn't relish a trip to the Emergency Room. Not to mention the hit her limited bank account would take in medical bills.

A knock on the door brought her head up, and she skipped over to answer it. She skewered the kids with a look that made them double time their clean-up efforts. By the time she'd greeted Vlad and escorted him to the room, it looked halfway presentable. Perhaps, someday, it would look all the way presentable.

"Hello, beautiful Thea. You are looking lovely today. How is Cuddles on this fine afternoon?"

Thea bounced over to Vlad and held her stuffed puppy up. "Cuddles is great. She was wondering if you were going to make any of the Russian tea cakes today with Yia Yia. Cuddles loves those."

Vlad chuckled and patted Cuddles on the head. "We will have to see what Yia Yia would like to make. I brought many ingredients."

Xander dribbled a small basketball on the floor, then shot it into the round basket he stored them in. "I think Yia Yia wants to play basketball today."

Xander got his pat on his head. "We might need to get some exercise after our cooking session. Where is your grandmother?"

"I'll get her," Xander yelled and tore off down the hall, his twin on his heels.

Vlad grinned, then focused on Eleni. "How are you today, Eleni? Our friend, Dean, stopped in yesterday to make sure I was aware of your peanut allergy. He was concerned about having nut oil anywhere in the building, especially around food you might eat or come in contact with."

Eleni nodded. "He saved me from some rogue peanut shells the other day. Hugh had been cracking them open on his desk and then handed me some papers they'd been lying on. Dean managed to grab them in time."

Vlad narrowed his eyes. "How does Hugh not know you have a peanut allergy?"

"You know Hugh. His mind is on more important things."

"It is a good thing Dean was there. He's a nice man to help you and go even further by checking with me. Seems he cares for you a good deal."

Eleni smiled, hoping her face wasn't as flushed as it felt. "Yes, he's a thoughtful person. Unfortunately, he almost got fired for standing up for me. Dean doesn't say much most of the time, but he stood up to Hugh in that instance. Luckily, Aarya walked in. She overheard most of the conversation and thanked Dean for his quick thinking and consideration."

"I'm not sure Dean would have been as insistent in our conversation if it was Reva with the allergy."

Eleni shrugged but didn't say anymore as her mom came down the hall.

"Vlad, so sorry to have made you wait. I was checking the internet for a few possible recipes and got distracted."

Vlad's face softened as he looked at Mom. "*You look beautiful, Georgina. I'm happy to wait.*" He signed the words as he said them. Eleni loved that he did this.

Mom blushed, then held out her hand. "Let's head to the kitchen. I set the computer up there."

Eleni ducked into the bathroom and quickly scrubbed around the toilet and sink, then wiped down the tub. What she wouldn't give to have a second bathroom someday. It would probably never happen, not with her salary. Too bad she couldn't have Reva's job. The woman made bank, and she spent much of her time flitting around the hotel, chatting with guests. Eleni could do that quite easily. And happily.

The twins scampered around the living room, attempting to peek into the kitchen to see what their grandmother and Vlad were up to. Eleni took the time to throw in another load of laundry and pull a few of the warmer weather clothes from her closet to make room for some sweaters. Oh, to have a closet that fit all of her wardrobe at once. The off-season stuff she put in under-the-bed boxes.

When she entered the dining room, she peered into the kitchen. Mom and Vlad sat at the table, the laptop open in front of them.

"*Did you find something good to try?*" She signed while she spoke so both understood her.

"We are learning some new signs to communicate better," Vlad said. "It's nice to learn them together. Much more fun."

"I'll teach them to you and the children later." Her mother lowered her eyes again to the screen. Eleni took the hint.

"*The kids wanted to go for a walk. Are you both okay here without us?*" She smirked at her mom.

Mom pursed her lips. "I think we can manage. Go have fun. We'll have something fabulous whipped up by the time you get back."

Thea and Xander whooped and scampered about when she told them to get their shoes on for a walk. Once they were ready, they said goodbye to their grandmother and Vlad and headed out.

"Which way should we walk? Remember it's Sunday and there might be some extra traffic on the main roads."

"Cuddles wants to walk that way." Thea pointed toward the crossroad that led to Dean's house.

Xander hopped up and down. "Yes, let's go that way. We can get an ice cream at Lickety Split."

"We'll see about that." Her budget didn't really lend itself to ice cream for three, but maybe if Dean happened to be around, she should buy him one as a thank you for potentially saving her life.

Checking her watch, she calculated when Dean might be arriving home. Much of it depended on if he got roped into doing more than his job description. Weddings fell under Chet's supervision and, fortunately, he planned his support staff adequately. Unlike Reva.

Eleni slowed her steps as they approached the house Dean lived in. His truck wasn't in the driveway. Disappointment flowed through her, but she smiled at her children.

"It's doesn't look like Mr. Dean is home yet. I told you he was probably working today."

Xander's shoulders drooped, but Thea's eyes opened wide as she pointed. "Look. There's his truck."

Eleni steered the twins to the side of the street as Dean pulled his truck into the driveway. He got out and swaggered their way, one eyebrow raising.

"Were you looking for me? Is everything okay?"

"We want you to come for ice cream with us," Xander shouted, and Thea nodded exuberantly.

Eleni rolled her eyes. "We were going for a walk to give Mom and Vlad some space to experiment with new recipes. I hadn't agreed to the ice cream yet, but I should probably buy you one for your heroic rescue yesterday."

A slight flush covered his cheeks, and he lowered his eyes for a second. "You're okay? You didn't have any adverse reactions to any of the peanut oil?"

"I'm pretty sure you wiped down every surface within a mile of my office, so no adverse reactions. Thank you."

"Did you want to come for ice cream, Mr. Dean?" Thea asked, dancing around with Cuddles.

Dean's eyebrows slanted together. "I love ice cream, but I haven't had dinner yet."

Both the twins giggled. "We didn't either."

Did he not want to join them? "You're welcome to come with us. I understand if you're tired after working all day, though. Please, don't feel you have to say yes."

Gazing down at his Ocean Pearl shirt, he tugged at the hem. "Let me change my shirt and I'd be happy to go. I've got an extra one right here." He reached into the cab of the truck and extracted a dark blue t-shirt. In seconds, he had the work shirt off and the new one on.

Eleni pivoted away when he changed but still got a glimpse of his bare chest. Oh, man, she wished she hadn't seen it. Dean Peters was extraordinary in many ways.

"All set," he said as he tossed his Ocean Pearl shirt on the front seat of the truck and shut the door. "Are we going to the ice cream place on Main Street?"

"Lickety Split is closest. Unless you'd rather walk all the way to the marina."

Dean took her elbow and steered her toward the center of town. "After working all day, I'd prefer not to do any more walking than I have to."

The kids skipped ahead, staying in sight of the adults as they strolled the few streets over to Main Street. Lickety Split was halfway down the road. Thea and Xander waited for them on the sidewalk outside.

Eleni waved at them. "Go on in and see what you want. We'll be right there."

The children scurried inside, and Dean held the door for her as they got closer. There was a small line, so they got in the queue and Eleni studied the board on the wall with all the flavors. Not that she needed to. She loved their Cookies and Cream and usually ended up with that.

"What's good here?"

She cocked her head. "Oh, everything. Haven't you been here yet?"

"No, I have a tendency to go to this little local place for dessert most nights. The proprietress is a terrific baker, and the ambiance beats any place I've ever been."

Heat rose to her cheeks, and Eleni focused on Thea and Xander. "You're up next. You may get a small cone each."

Xander ordered Double Fudge Swirl and Thea got Peppermint Stick. They knew enough not to order something with nuts.

"I'll have a small Cookies and Cream in a sugar cone, please. And whatever this gentleman is having. It's all together."

"Hmm, I think I'll try the Black Raspberry, please. Same size."

Eleni glanced up. "You can get something bigger if you want. I just know the kids won't eat anything more than a small."

"Small is fine." He pulled out a twenty-dollar bill and set it on the counter. Eleni tried to hand it back. She had a few smaller bills in her hand ready to go.

"You can pay for my cone, but I insist on covering the rest. It's only fair after you feed me dessert almost every night." He took one of her small bills, then handed the twenty to the server, who giggled at their exchange. She was a high school girl who often worked at the resort during the busy summer months. More color filled Eleni's cheeks.

They stood aside as another family moved up to order. Once the ice cream was ready and they all had napkins, they headed to an outdoor table to eat their treats.

Eleni perused the seating area, the small town feel of the place warming her even though she was eating something cold. She and the kids, along with Dean, made a nice family unit and anyone who didn't know them might automatically assume that's what they were.

Dean hadn't been here long, but Eleni allowed herself to wonder if she could ever have this complete family scene again. And if Dean would be the one filling in the role of dad.

CHAPTER EIGHT

*G*ripping the small paper bag tightly in his hand, Dean strode the last few steps to Eleni's house. No one was in the yard, and he debated waiting outside for someone to see him or should he simply go up and knock on the door? Standing around outside seemed too stalkerish, especially since he had an actual reason for being here today. Other than hoping he'd get dessert and see Eleni.

He'd barely rapped his knuckles on the door when Xander tugged it open and squealed, "Mr. Dean is here. Mom!"

Eleni's laughter rang through the house. "Well, let him in."

As Dean followed Xander down past the living room, Eleni appeared in the kitchen doorway. "Have you eaten yet? We got a late start tonight. It's only chicken tacos."

"Um, I had a sandwich before I came over." He wouldn't tell her it only had one slice of turkey in it because he'd run out.

"Oh, that isn't much. I'm sure you can manage to choke down a taco or two."

Georgina stood. "You can have my seat. I snacked on the chicken all afternoon."

He started to object, but she took his hand and led him to her chair, then whispered in his ear, "This way I get dessert before anyone else."

How could he argue with that? Making sure he had her attention, he signed, "*thank you*".

Eleni had gotten another plate and set it in front of him. "Taco shells are right there, along with all the fixings. Help yourself. We aren't formal here."

He'd figured that out the few times he'd been inside her house. Small bowls of lettuce, chopped up tomatoes, onions, cheese, and seasoned chicken littered the table. A jar of salsa sat front and center with a spoon inside. He wasn't sure he'd ever been to a place where you had to put your own taco together. There was a first time for everything.

Dean placed the paper bag onto the table next to Eleni's plate. She eyed him strangely. "What's this?"

"Something you need." He didn't elaborate, just took a soft taco shell and began to fill it with ingredients.

Eleni took a bite of the taco she'd already filled, then peeked in the bag. Her eyes popped open, and she finished chewing quickly. "Where did you get an Epi Pen? These things are a million dollars. It's not yours, is it? I'm not taking something you need."

Dean took his time nibbling on the stuff falling from the end of his taco. "I have a good friend who's a pharmaceutical rep. I called and asked if there was any way to get them cheaper. He said he had a few they couldn't sell because the labels were placed incorrectly."

"He just gave it to you? How the heck do they justify wasting something so essential?"

Dean shrugged. He wasn't sure where Maggie got it from, but she had contacts for things he didn't even know about. She'd mumbled something about the first aid kits in each resort and said it wasn't a problem. "I had him overnight it to me, so you wouldn't be without for long. What happened a few days ago scared me. I don't want you to ever be without one of these."

Eleni patted his hand, and her face softened. "That's so sweet, Dean. I really appreciate it. Let me know the cost of the overnight shipping, and I'll at least pay you for that."

He was about to tell her to forget it, but Eleni was a proud woman and liked to earn everything she got. More people needed to be like her. "Because it's small, it was only about ten dollars. Slightly under."

She took another bite of her taco, then tucked the Epi Pen in her purse. When she returned to the table, she handed him a ten-dollar bill. It killed him to take it since she needed this money far more than he did. He'd find a way to get it back to her, plus more if he could.

The kids chatted away about some of the Halloween festivities the island had every year and how excited they were about their costumes. From the sound of it, Eleni helped them make the costumes, instead of buying something from the store.

Dean only had one taco since he didn't want to eat too much of Eleni's food. Not that she'd mind—her generosity was endless. But he couldn't justify taking what little she had. He'd already put a bug in Trey's ear about making new mandates for staffing and salaries based on the information he'd accumulated in the past eight weeks.

He brought his plate to the sink and rinsed it. Xander raced from his seat to do the same.

"Do you want to play basketball, Mr. Dean? I've been practicing."

Dean smiled down at the exuberant boy. "Don't practice too much. I finally almost caught up to how good the rest of you are."

"If we play, then you'll be practicing, too."

"Ask your mom first. I don't know if you've got homework or chores to do." Eleni didn't put unrealistic expectations on her children, but she did require them to be responsible for their toys and clothes and do some of the easier tasks around the house. Even though he and Trey had been raised in luxury, his parents had been all about having responsibilities and consequences.

As Xander raced off to ask his mom, Dean watched the family unit. He felt blessed to be included in some of their home time. They'd never made him feel like an outsider or that he was in the way.

The boy was back in a flash, nodding like a bobblehead. "She said yes, but only as long as you're here. If you have to leave, I need to come in."

Dean waved to Eleni, who was reaching for another taco. Knowing her, she'd most likely been attending to some other chore that needed to be done while the rest of the family had started eating.

"Send Thea out, too, if she wants, when she's done."

The girl munched on her taco while petting Cuddles in her lap. Eleni sent him a grateful smile. He'd do anything for her if she looked at him that way.

Xander grabbed the basketball and started dribbling under the hoop. It sat next to the street on the border of their yard and the generous neighbor who let them use it.

"Have you ever been in the military, Mr. Dean?"

Where had that comment come from? He took a few steps over to Xander. "See how I don't always walk straight. I had an accident when I was little, and it made one leg a tiny bit shorter than the other. That's something that makes it hard to be in the military."

Xander cocked his head. "My Uncle Thaddeus is in the army. His legs are the same size, I guess."

"Do you see him often?" How was he related to them? Or was this someone they only called uncle but was more a friend of Eleni's?

"Not really. He comes here sometimes at Christmas, but I wish he was here more. To help Mom because my dad isn't here to help her."

"Your mom seems very self-sufficient to me. I'll be she can do most of the stuff a guy might do."

Xander's eyes gazed at the darkening sky. "I guess, but I'm not big enough to do some of this stuff, and Uncle Thaddeus isn't here."

"Is he your mom's brother or your dad's brother?" Eleni hadn't mentioned getting any help from her late husband's family.

"Mom's brother and Yia Yia's other kid. She has a boy and girl, also, but not twins like me and Thea. Uncle Thaddeus is younger than mom. Since my dad died, I'm the man of the house, but I don't know how to do that and sometimes things scare me."

"Your mom is a capable lady. I'm sure she can take care of most things."

The anxious eyes that stared at him made Dean want to pull the boy into his arms. "What about if something happens to Mom? I heard her tell Yia Yia about the peanuts at work the other day. That's why you brought her a new medicine pen, right? If she got sick, I'd have to take care of everything."

Dean caught the ball Xander had been dribbling and lowered himself to the child's level. "You're only eight, Xander. No one expects you to take over the family. If something did happen to your mom, your grandmother would be around. Even if she can't hear, she's still a smart lady and would know who to contact to get help."

Xander bit his lip and dropped his head. "Would you help us, Mr. Dean? I mean, if Mom got sick or needed help."

No child should have to worry about this stuff. "If you ever need help, all you have to do is ask. Or let me know if you're upset about something. Okay?"

The boy's shoulders relaxed, and his face brightened. "Really? Thanks. Do you think you could help teach me some stuff that a dad would help a kid do?"

"Like what?"

Xander shrugged and stared at the ground again. "Just father and son stuff." He kicked a stone on the street and watched as it skittered away.

Father and son? Xander was looking for a father figure. Someone to look up to and lean on and learn from. Dean had never seen himself in that role, for good reason. Now, he wondered if he had it in him to be a good role model for a kid.

Patting Xander on the shoulders, he said, "That might be kind of fun. I don't have any kids of my own, so I haven't done anything like that. But if you think I might be okay at it, then I'm happy to step in."

"You'll be great at it," Xander yelled. "You already play basketball and hang out sometimes. This'll be really cool. Thanks."

Dean was almost knocked over as Xander launched himself into his arms. The way he clung so tightly to his waist, Dean had a feeling this had been eating away at the boy for a while. What would Eleni think of him stepping in to do dad stuff? And would she want him to step up and take over some of the duties her deceased husband had done? He didn't even know what to think about that possibility.

The worst part of working the overnight shifts wasn't how tired Dean was. It wasn't even that he got to witness spoiled vacationers, ones who could afford the luxury suites at this resort, acting like idiots from too much drink or a desire to be young again. Mostly, it was that Eleni wasn't here.

In the last two months, he'd come to expect her generous smile and kind words asking how he was. The lunch she often brought to share wasn't expected, but the fact she usually ate it with him was nice.

He'd never stopped working to eat before. Often, Maggie warmed something up for him and brought it to his office, leaving it on his side table because he was embroiled in some urgent matter.

He laughed, remembering how ridiculous his schedule was, how he thought the entire company would fall apart if he didn't put in twelve-hour days. Since he'd been here, he'd relied on his department heads far more than he ever had. Surprisingly, none of them had complained one bit. A few had actually thanked him for allowing them more autonomy and trusting them to do their jobs. Why he hadn't before, he didn't have a clue.

Okay, maybe he did. He was a bit of a control freak and hadn't wanted to let go of the reins in case the job wasn't done correctly. While here, he'd had to rely on his staff more than ever. They'd stepped up to the plate and taken their responsibilities seriously and with confidence and skill.

As he pushed his cart down the hallway, his biggest staff hiring regret strolled down the hallway in his direction. Hugh, and he didn't look happy.

The man narrowed his eyes and crossed his arms as Dean approached, hoping to simply pass on by. No such luck.

"I know it was you who tattled to corporate about the peanut incident."

Dean didn't have the energy to deal with a temper tantrum at the moment. Taking a deep breath, he replied, "Right, because I'm in tight with the Petrakis brothers. That's why I'm cleaning up sand and vomit from the floors."

The words were disrespectfully said, and Dean would have dressed down any employee who spoke to *him* that way. Yet Hugh's less than stellar performance in his job had Dean making an exception.

Hugh's jaw tightened. "I'll be keeping my eye on you, Peters. I may have to dig a little and see why you got ousted from the Cape Cod resort, but if I find any kind of dirt, you may find yourself in need of new employment."

Dean merely stared at Hugh, a tiny smile on his face. The man wouldn't find any dirt, hidden or otherwise. Maggie had set up his background impeccably with the Cape resort.

With Dean's silence, Hugh's face turned redder. "Listen, you don't want to tick me off. You'll find yourself pulling night duty for the next six months. Do you understand?"

"Yes, sir." Dean kept his tone respectful when he wanted to fire the man on the spot.

"I'm leaving at eleven tonight, but I'll be checking on your progress to make sure you finished everything on your list."

Everything on Dean's lists always got done. Hugh knew that as well as he did, so the threat was ridiculous. "If that's all, sir, I'll get working on that list."

"You do that." Hugh threw him another glare, then sauntered to the registration desk where two pretty young ladies stood helping guests.

Being Friday night, the desk would stay busy for a while as people came in and out, needing last minute items they'd forgotten or requesting special services. Room service stayed open until two, and often Dean was asked to retrieve the trays outside the rooms after the guests were done. The food waste he saw made him sick when he thought of Eleni and her family and how frugally they lived.

Dean kept his eye on Hugh as the man flirted with each of the women at the desk. Both had to be at least fifteen years younger than the assistant manager, yet they flirted right back, batting their eyelashes and swinging their hair over their shoulders. Fortunately, the man kept his hands to himself, because Dean couldn't overlook something that disgusting.

Once Hugh left, Dean set a course for behind the desk to empty the trash. The blonde—Ashley, he thought her name was—waved and smiled. The other one, Monica, sat on her stool and looked bored.

"Gets tiring at night, huh?"

Monica rolled her eyes but remained quiet. Guess the maintenance guy wasn't powerful enough or paid enough to merit preferential treatment.

"The assistant manager seems to like you both. There must be perks to that."

Ashley laughed and made a face, flipping her hair over her shoulder. "The guy's a pig, but if we don't giggle and make him feel important, he gets all sulky. Since he schedules our hours, it's best to make him happy."

Dean scowled as he tied up the bag of trash. "Have you ever thought of letting the manager know? Or going to corporate with your complaints?"

"Right," Ashley said. "Because Hugh wouldn't find out who it was and either fire us or make our lives miserable. It's easier to flirt and make him think he's all that."

"I'm sorry. You shouldn't have to put up with it."

Monica rolled her eyes again. "Whatever. He lets us come back and use the pool sometimes if it isn't busy."

Dean mulled that over as he went about the rest of his duties that night. It wasn't a bad incentive to working here, but did they want over a hundred employees using the pool at all times?

Once two o'clock had come and gone, Dean rolled his cart and parked it next to the employee bathroom near the main office. Letting himself into the outer room where Eleni worked, he glanced back to make sure no one was paying any attention. The place was as quiet as a library during spring break.

Not that he had to worry too much. People really didn't notice him and what he was doing. It was like he blended in with the wallpaper.

He quickly perused Aarya's desk for any signs she wasn't the loyal employee she appeared to be. Everything was in tip top shape and super organized. Hugh's desk was another matter. Sticky notes littered the surface, which would have been great, except many of them were from Eleni or Aarya reminding him of jobs he needed to do. Ones Dean knew he hadn't done yet. Once his reconnaissance here was finished, he and Trey would have to have a good long chat with Hugh about his future with the company.

Aside from Dean's fake file resting on the side of Hugh's desk, there wasn't anything suspicious there. Honestly, Hugh was so lackadaisical at his job, Dean wondered if he'd have the energy to acquire the marketing information and sell it.

In the guise of straightening up and dusting, Dean checked out the business office, the marketing office, and then both Chet and Reva's offices which were next to each other on the main floor.

He'd been in Reva's office before, but if it was during the day, she usually kicked the barrel toward him and said, "Here, take it."

Tonight, he spent a little more time examining the items placed on the many surfaces in the room. Quite a few of them were pictures of her and Trey. On a boat. Near the pool. Drinking at the beach snack shack. All of them made it seem like she and Trey were tight. Romantic. In love.

The poor sap actually thought Trey would settle down with her at some point. Sleeping with him any time he wanted was hardly the way to get his attention. His brother had a lady, or two or three, in every port. If Reva was holding out hope that Demitrius Petrakis would get down on one knee and pledge his everlasting love, she was in for a big surprise.

CHAPTER NINE

*E*leni clapped her hands and got the attention of the kids sitting at the table. "Livy, Kandra, your mom just pulled up. Start getting your stuff together. Xander and Thea, please make sure to clean up the mess in the living room."

Livy tipped her head. "We should help clean that up, too. Ms. Eleni. Thea and Xander didn't make it all by themselves and shouldn't have to do it all."

"That's very sweet of you, Livy. I'll go outside and chat with your mom until you finish up."

The kids all grinned. It was their way of getting a bit more time to play together while the moms got some adult conversation.

Nadine relaxed in one of the chairs in the yard as Eleni came out with two cups of tea. She knew the drill. "What kind of a mess did they leave today?"

Eleni shook her head. "You don't even want to know. The science project they did required every Lego and block we owned. It could be a while."

Nadine laughed and sipped her tea. Both women let out a deep sigh.

"Don't forget about the barbecue this weekend. I know you have to work Friday and Saturday, but I was hoping you could come even for a little while. Get your mother out of the house, too."

"Oh, Mom is absolutely looking forward to it. Once she heard Vlad was planning to bring some of his tasty treats, she started rifling through her wardrobe for a suitable outfit."

"Georgie is so darned cute. She and Vlad are great together. Have they admitted to being more than friends yet?"

Eleni rolled her eyes. "Not to me. And since we're usually around the house, they certainly haven't had a chance to be more than that."

"What about you?"

Eleni cocked her head. "What do you mean me?"

"Have you had a chance to be more than friends with anyone lately?"

Her laugh rang across the yard. "When would I have time for that?"

"Maybe not yet, but why don't you start by inviting that handsome man from work to the party Friday night?"

"Handsome man from work? Where did you get that idea?" She had a feeling she knew who'd tattled on Dean's visits.

"Your children have mentioned a gentleman who stops by for dessert at times. Someone you work with."

Eleni huffed. "It's just dessert. He lives around the corner, and I think he gets lonely at times. He comes over and plays basketball with the kids and has dessert."

"According to the kids, it's almost every night. What's going on between you two?"

Hiding behind her teacup, Eleni gave herself a moment to figure out what to say. "Nothing that I know of. I'm nice to him, and he's nice to me and the kids and Mom. He's only been on the island a few months. He doesn't really know many people."

"Then, bring him to the party. It's the perfect opportunity to introduce him to others."

Would Dean want that? "I don't know. He's kind of reserved and quiet. I'm not sure if it's shyness or just a desire to not get involved. It took a while before I got him to say more than a few words to me at a time."

Nadine smirked. "Maybe he just doesn't know anyone. What better way to introduce him to the neighborhood?"

Eleni pictured Nadine and Marek's house across the street from the ocean. "We don't live in your neighborhood."

Waving her hand, Nadine snorted. "The island isn't that big. I consider everyone here a neighbor."

"Okay, I'll ask him. Or better yet, I'll have the kids ask him. He seems to be unable to say no to them."

"But he can say no to you?"

She shrugged. "I haven't really asked him for much. Except a chair with better lumbar support. He found one for me."

"Your charm is working already. I'd love to meet him. And once we get him acquainted with a few others, we can start doing some couples stuff."

"Couples stuff? We aren't a couple, Nadine. I'm not sure what we are, but there hasn't been anything romantic between us." Unless she counted holding his hand.

"Yet. We'll get you there. Then, we can have a few nights and hang out at either J Roger or listen to the singers at Sundown."

It had been forever since Eleni had gone to listen to people play their guitars and sing at the restaurant near the pier. She liked Sundown, because it wasn't the kind of bar where the sole purpose of going there was to drink. Since she'd realized Sean was an alcoholic, she'd stopped having alcohol of any kind.

"Xander wants me to bring brownies to your party. I hope that's okay. Unless there's something else you need."

"Brownies are good. Mostly, I just want my friends there. And friends of friends. So bring Dean. That's his name, right?"

"Yes, Dean Peters. I'll ask him and see what he says, but I won't force him. I'll gently encourage him."

"Tell him you're bringing your brownies, and if he wants dessert Friday night, that's where they'll be. A little subterfuge is never a bad thing. Or use guilt. You provide him with dessert most nights. The least he can do is escort you to a friend's house for a few hours."

Nadine tipped her head, her lips curling up in a grin. She reached for her tea and finished off the cup just as the kids exploded from the house into the yard.

"Hey, Mom, we made the coolest habitats for some of the island animals today," Kandra said.

Nadine eyed Eleni. "The blocks?"

"Mmhmm. Lots of blocks. Are they all picked up and put away?" Eleni addressed the children.

"Yep," the four of them yelled together.

"Great." Nadine rose to her feet and pointed at the school bags on the ground. "Make sure you have everything you need and let's get going. I hope your father already got supper cooking. I'm starving."

As Nadine and the girls got in the car and drove off, Eleni thought how nice it was that Nadine had a husband who got dinner ready. Not that she could complain. Her mom often had the food ready to go by the time Eleni returned from work.

An image of Dean standing at the stove with an apron around his trim hips appeared in her mind. She bit her lip to keep from laughing. But if they ever got to the point where Dean was making dinner for them, she knew she wouldn't be laughing. She'd be down on her knees giving thanks.

"You're coming tonight, right?"

Dean glanced up from the mulch he was placing in the flower beds in the garden patio. Eleni stood above him, her hands on her hips, a hopeful smile on her lips.

"I'm kind of filthy right now. I smell like tree bark."

Glancing at her watch, she pursed her lips. "Yes, but you get off in a half hour at five. I work until six. That gives you an hour longer than me to take a shower and get ready. You don't even have to share your bathroom with three other people."

Dean wanted to back out, but Eleni and her family had been so good to him in the two months since he'd been here, he hated to disappoint them. Of course, a local barbecue with lots of people wasn't really his thing.

"How many people will be there?"

"Not many. Maybe twenty-five or thirty."

His eyebrows went up. "That's your idea of not many? And the only ones I'll know are you, Georgie, and the kids."

"You can stay by my side the whole night. I'll even hold your hand if you get scared."

If only she'd do that. Last week when she'd told him about her husband, he'd taken it and held it the entire walk back. He hadn't stayed once they'd gotten to her place. There was too much guilt eating away at him for lying to her. Exactly what she'd said she couldn't forgive her deceased husband for.

But what choice did he have? *You could tell her the truth.* But how did he know he could trust her not to warn Aarya or Hugh or any of the other suspects? In his heart, he knew she couldn't be the culprit. If she was, she clearly hadn't gotten any money from the deal. Not if her financial woes were anything to go by. She was loyal. Probably more so to her immediate bosses than to him. He didn't want her acting differently if she found out now. The truth would eventually come out once he found the person responsible.

"Fine, I'll go. Do I need to bring anything? I can pick up some chips and salsa at the market."

"I think Nadine and Marek are pretty much set, but if you feel you need to bring something, a bag of chips won't go bad."

"What time again and where?" He'd taken some drives around the island on his days off, but there were still some areas he wasn't familiar with.

"Seven-thirty. They live over by Sandpiper Point, but you can come with us."

"Okay, that's good. I'll come to your house. Is seven early enough?"

"That should give us plenty of time to get there, assuming I can get the kids ready in time. Gotta get back to the grind. I'm sure Hugh will have a million things for me to do before I go."

Dean stood and reached out, but his hand was a mess, so he stopped just shy of her arm. "Don't let Hugh talk you into anything that keeps you late or that *he* should be doing. He's the assistant manager. Let him manage."

Eleni rolled her eyes and laughed. "Sure, that'll go over well. But he knows I can't bend on my scheduled time because of the kids. Aarya has given me permission to drop everything and walk out when the clock hits six. Hugh is aware of this. I'll see you later. I think you'll enjoy some of the people there tonight."

Dean watched as she went back inside, then dug back into the mulch. If he was going to be at Eleni's house by seven and take a shower, plus run to the market for chips, he'd need to get out of work on time, also. That wasn't something he was good at, but tonight he'd ensure he did.

At exactly two minutes past five, he clocked out and jumped in his truck. He drove to work even though it was only a few miles to his house. Eleni lived around the corner from him and often rode her bike. It made him feel lazy, but he hadn't been on a bike since the accident when he was ten. Doubtful, he ever would again, no matter how many people used that as their mode of transportation on the island.

He showered quickly, threw on a newer pair of jeans and a long-sleeved t-shirt, then rushed to the market for two bags of chips and a jar of salsa. Ridiculous when he could afford to cater dinner for the entire island.

The walk to Eleni's didn't take long, but he took his time, knowing she'd only gotten home a short while ago. Was she the type who was always late? Not if her work ethic was anything to go by.

Thea and Xander sat at the outside table, rolling a small ball back and forth. Georgie stood inside at the kitchen sink, washing something. He waved as he approached the yard. The kids rushed toward him and almost knocked him over with their hugs. They'd begun to do that in the last week, and he wasn't sure how he felt about it. Embracing them back, he couldn't deny it was a nice feeling. One he hadn't experienced in many years. Far too many to count.

Georgie trotted down the steps and gave him a quick hug as well. "I'm so glad you're coming with us. At least one person will look at me while they talk, so I can understand."

"*I'll talk to you all night,*" he said, doing the few signs he remembered. He'd never been a social butterfly like his brother and much preferred staying home and reading or watching TV.

When Eleni came onto the porch, he held his breath. At work, she usually wore dressy pants, but tonight she had on a pastel sundress and carried a sweater over her arm. The fabric swirled around her curves, teasing him.

"Thea, Xander, come give me a hand with these brownies. You wanted them, so you have to help carry them."

"I can help." Dean stepped forward, reaching for the plastic container.

Eleni smiled. "No, I need you for more manly things. The cooler in the kitchen has soda and juice boxes for the kids. Can you bring that to the car, please?"

Once the food and drinks were in the trunk of her sedan, they all climbed in. Georgie insisted she ride in the back with the kids. Dean thought about asking to drive, but he had no idea where they were going.

The ride didn't take long, but when they arrived, the number of vehicles parked on the street made him nervous. Was there anyone here who knew his true identity? Someone he'd met before or had somehow seen a picture of him? He made it a point not to be photographed by any media if he could help it, but you could never be too careful.

With the cooler hefted in his arms, he followed Eleni and her family to the side of the house and around back. The place wasn't on the beach, but it was across the street from an access road. The backyard was filled with more people than he ever wanted to be with.

"Put the cooler by the shed, please. You're welcome to anything in it, Dean. But there's nothing alcoholic. I'm sure Marek has beer, if you want one."

After depositing the cooler, Dean reached out and took Eleni's hand, tugging her near. "I don't need any of that. Just seeing how pretty you look gives me a buzz."

Her cheeks flushed, and that beautiful smile crossed her face. "That's very sweet. Do you charm all the ladies like that? I'll have to watch you tonight."

"No charm for anyone but you. Granted, no one else is as pretty as you."

She pursed her lips and narrowed her eyes. "Oh, you're looking for a *few* brownies tonight, aren't you? Keep it up, and I'll have to bake a whole batch just for you."

If only Eleni knew he rarely dated or the length of time it had been since he'd had sex. She wouldn't be worried about him having a roving eye. Now, if Trey was here, that would be an entirely different story.

Squeezing his hand, Eleni drew him into the crowd of people. "Let me introduce you to our hosts."

They approached an attractive couple in their mid-thirties. With their dark coloring and curly hair, he assumed they were the parents of the kids Eleni helped to homeschool.

"Hey, I want you to meet Dean Peters. He works at The Pearl with me. Dean, this is Nadine and Marek Tali. You've met their girls, Kandra and Livy."

Dean stuck his hand out, and Marek shook it. "Good to meet you, mate. Glad you could make it."

The accent took Dean by surprise. "Australian?"

Marek cocked his head and grinned. "Close enough. I'm from Papua New Guinea."

Looking at Nadine, he asked, "You, too?"

Nadine laughed. "Oh, no, I'm as American as apple pie. We met when I did a year teaching abroad in his country."

Marek tucked his wife into his shoulder and kissed her head. "Love at first sight."

"Not for me." Nadine shook her loose curls. "I needed a few months of serious romancing before he began to grow on me."

"Good thing she finally fell for me. I was running out of things to charm her with."

When Nadine gazed at her husband, though, it was obvious she was thoroughly charmed.

"Your girls are lovely and very polite. I've met them a few times when Eleni's teaching them and stops at The Pearl."

"Glad they were on their best behavior." Marek inclined his head toward the kitchen. "Make sure you help yourself to anything here. Plenty of munchies and drinks. I'll be throwing the meat on the grill soon."

Dean got dragged behind Eleni again as she introduced him to more of the guests. He'd never remember their names. They all seemed nice and welcomed him to the island, but he stayed next to Eleni's side for most of the night.

His gaze roamed the yard making sure Georgie wasn't by herself. He shouldn't have worried. The Pearl's head chef, Vlad, stood next to her, showing her something on his phone. Georgie often used her phone, so people could type on it if she couldn't get what they were saying. But the smile on Vlad's face was quite clear. No interpretation needed. Dean couldn't blame the man, Georgie was adorable. Just like her daughter.

Eleni finished the last bite of her potato salad and wiped her hands on a napkin. Dean rose to his feet and held his hand out. "Let me throw that away for you."

The smile she sent warmed him, even in the cooler ocean air. "The trash cans are behind that section of tall fence. Thanks."

Grabbing his own plate, he hoofed it to the cans and tossed them in. Children's laughter rang his way, and he peeked around the wooden obstruction. Thea and Livy sat on the ground with another child, all playing with stuffed puppies.

"Dean says Cuddles is the most beautiful dog he's ever seen." Thea held her dog up for show.

"Dean?" The other child said. "Is that the guy with your mom? Who is he?"

He didn't dare move now. Not that he wanted to spy on the kids, but he didn't want them embarrassed that he'd overheard them.

"He works with my mom. He's cool and plays basketball with us after supper sometimes."

Cool? Not sure he'd ever heard that word to describe him. He'd take it.

"Is he gonna marry your mom?" Livy asked.

Thea shrugged. "I don't know. He probably should, so he doesn't have to walk home every night by himself."

Dean chuckled at the child's reasoning. Often, he didn't want to walk home.

The other girl pranced her dog over to Cuddles. "My mom said she'd only get married again if the guy was really rich. Is Dean rich?"

"Mom says he's poor."

Dean's heart sank. Is that how Eleni saw him? Was he only a charity case to her? Wasn't that a kick in the pants with the amount of money he had?

"But we're rich, because we have lots of family and love. Dean doesn't have anyone. So we're letting him share some of our rich. Mama says there's nothing better than love and family."

The words Thea spoke had him melting against the fence. Rich in love and family. Something that had never occurred to him. On the other hand, being with Eleni, Georgie, and the kids, he could definitely see it. He'd wondered how Eleni could be so upbeat and giving when she had so little, but her daughter just explained it in spades.

CHAPTER TEN

Where had Dean disappeared to? Eleni craned her neck to search the area but only saw Xander running around with one of his friends who lived next door. Oh, there he was. He had a strange look on his face.

She met him halfway across the yard. "Did you get lost?"

A half smile lifted one side of his mouth. "No, just watching Thea play with her friends. She's such a sweet kid. You've done an amazing job raising her and Xander."

"Why, thank you, kind sir. I like to think I did okay, but it's nice to hear from other people. And you've seen them at their worst sometimes, tired, cranky, and at home when they don't feel the need to use their best manners."

He stroked his fingers down her bare arm, sending shivers along her spine. "Even tired and cranky, they're good kids."

He stared at her intensely, and Eleni forgot where they were. Had her husband ever looked at her that way? Without a doubt, no other man ever had. She reached out to take his hand when a large yellow dog ran in between them.

Dean stepped back, concern on his face. Eleni bent to pat the dog, who sat nudging her hand.

"Hey, Boomer. Did you get away from Ben again?" The lab sat on his hind legs and lifted his paws in the air. "Good boy."

"A friend of yours?" Dean asked, his body stiff.

"Oh, God, Eleni. I'm so sorry." A tall, dark-haired man trotted over, followed by a blonde woman, a bit younger than them. "He thinks he's the guest of honor and needs to personally greet everyone."

"That's very sociable of him. Ben, Kat, let me introduce you to Dean Peters, a friend of mine." When she twisted toward Dean, he stood still, his eyes never leaving the canine. Was he afraid of dogs?

She took his hand and urged him closer. "This is Kat Worthington and Ben Hadley. Ben's a master carpenter here on the island, and Kat helps her grandmother with Secondhand Antiques and Sandpiper Bed and Breakfast."

"I have a real job, too," Kat said, shaking Dean's hand. "Luckily, I can do it remotely and spend more time with Gran. And Ben." Her eyes moved toward the handsome guy at her side.

"An antique store? Does it do well on the island?" Dean asked.

"Well enough," Kat replied. "We have more than antiques. Right now, we're piled high with fall decorations like pumpkins, cornstalks, hay bales, gourds, apple cider, and pie. Eleni we're expecting a good-sized crowd over the next few weekends, if you want to bake some of your famous apple pie for us. It's always a big seller."

"You sell your apple pie?" Dean tipped his head. Did he think it wasn't good enough to sell?

"Yes, and you always eat seconds and thirds, so I think it's fine for the public."

Shaking his head, Dean scowled. "Oh, I didn't mean it wasn't. It's the best I've ever had. I hope you ask top dollar for it."

Kat laughed. "We certainly don't give it away. It helps us, and it helps Eleni. You should bring the kids this weekend to get pumpkins.

We just got a delivery this afternoon. I know you wanted some hay bales, as well, for your yard."

"I do. If it gets too busy and they fly off the shelves, put two aside for me, will you? I work tomorrow, so I won't be able to get there until Sunday."

"You've got it," Ben said, scratching his dog behind the ears. "Boomer will guard them himself."

The dog shuffled on his feet, and Ben clipped a leash to his collar. "First, he needs a walk. Nice meeting you, Dean. We'll see you later, Eleni."

The couple left, and Eleni sidled closer to Dean. "Do you need a walk? We can take a stroll on the beach to get away from the crowd for a bit."

His shoulders relaxed as he nodded. "Can we? What about the kids?"

"I'll let my mom know to keep her eyes peeled. Be back in a sec."

Her mom waved her off once she told her where she was going. "Take your time, dear. It's been a while since you've had a beach walk with a handsome man."

A while. Probably more than five years. Sean hadn't been much for romantic walks on the sand once they'd gotten married and had the kids.

"Ready, sir?" Eleni held out her arm.

Dean linked his through hers. "As I'll ever be. Lead on. I'm not sure the best way to get there."

Escorting him across the street to the path, Eleni chatted about some of the people at the party and how long they'd been on the island. Dean was a good listener, and she hoped she wasn't boring him. At least, he asked questions now and then, so she knew he heard her.

"Would you like to come get pumpkins with us on Sunday?"

"That's your family time. I wouldn't want to intrude."

"You hang out with us enough, you might as well be family. You're welcome to come."

Was that too bold of her? What exactly did she want from her relationship with him? Did they even have a relationship? Friends, without question, but now they were holding hands. It was a first step. Would they ever take a second?

"Do you need me to come?"

"Need you?" The more he hung around, the more she thought she did.

He puffed up his chest and made fists. "You know for my manly muscles. Lifting things up and putting them down."

She made a point of eyeing his muscles. "I think we'd manage without you if we had to. On the other hand, it sure would make things easier if you were there. I'd love to get a really big pumpkin this year, but I'd never be able to get it in and out of the car. You can get a pumpkin for your place, too."

"I don't have any place to put one. My apartment is over the garage, and I don't have a porch, just a stoop. With my luck, I'd trip over it and fall down the stairs."

"We can't have that, can we?" She paused in her step to face him. "I appreciate the help if you could come. I'll even throw in an apple pie."

Dean slipped his hand into her hair and tucked it behind her ear. The breeze blew it back out again. The moon was up and almost full, lighting up the sky, illuminating the water and waves as they crashed onto shore.

He gazed at her with that intense look again, and she wished she could interpret it.

"You don't have to bribe me with anything." His thumb stroked her cheek. "I like doing things that make you happy, Eleni. You've made my time here so much better than I ever imagined."

She was about to respond when his thumb grazed her bottom lip, freezing any words before they could slip out. His head lowered, and she watched mesmerized. Waiting for his lips to touch hers. *Oh, please.*

"Your wish is my command."

Had she said her plea aloud? It didn't matter, because he finally kissed her. Soft, gentle, and over too quickly. She skimmed her hands up his chest to rest on his shoulders. Firm, rugged, and perfect for holding onto.

When she rose on her toes, he met her halfway and pressed his lips to her again. It had been too long since she'd felt like this, swept away with longing and desire.

He drew her tighter to his chest, and she deepened the kiss. It didn't take much coaxing before he joined in just as fiercely. His hand skated up her back, stopping to hold her neck as they continued the dance.

A dog barking in the distance grew louder. It got her attention, so she eased back. "I don't think we're alone."

"Unfortunately." It was the only word he spoke. He draped his arm around her shoulder and started walking again. It was a companionable silence. She wished she could ask him to kiss her again.

When they returned to the party, many of the guests had left. Thea and Xander both whined when she told them it was time to go. The thought of not being with Dean had a similar effect on her.

Dean instructed her to go straight home. He'd walk to his place once he'd helped her unload her car, which worked out when Thea fell asleep on the ride and needed to be carried inside.

Once the kids and Georgie were in the house and the car unloaded, Dean wished them all good night. Eleni escorted him to the porch.

"Can I walk you home?" She wanted to spend more time with him.

Dean smiled, that sexy one that drove her crazy. "Then, I'd just have to walk you back here.'

"Okay, sounds good."

Dean laughed. "I'll say good night now."

She stepped into his arms, and he immediately enveloped her in his embrace. It was heaven.

"You did a great job tonight. I know lots of people aren't your thing, but you got through it."

He framed her face with his rough hands. "Because of you. You have a way of making everything all right. Thank you."

His head lowered, and she held her breath waiting for another dazzling kiss. But his lips merely brushed across hers, once, then swiftly a second time. Straightening, he spun and strode away.

At the bottom of the stairs, he peeked over his shoulder. "I'll see you Sunday."

After that kiss, Eleni wasn't sure she'd make it until Sunday.

Dean pulled his old pick up in front of Eleni's house and beeped. As he exited the vehicle, Xander and Thea flew out of the house, straight for him. He braced himself on his good leg and waited, arms out. They both jumped, and he swung them around for a rotation, then set them down again.

"Ready to go pick some pumpkins?"

"I'm gonna get one that's bigger than me." Xander held out his arms wide.

Thea threw him a sister look. "Mom said we could each get a medium-sized one and one big one for the porch."

Her brother scrunched up his face. "Well, the big one can be bigger than me."

"I don't know." Dean placed his hand on the boy's head. "I think you've grown just since I saw you Friday night. What have you been eating?"

"I had broccoli for supper last night. Two helpings. And apples. Apples are excellent for you."

Thea laughed. "You had apple pie. I don't think that counts as good for you."

Dean snickered, too. "If it's your mom's apple pie, it's very good for you."

"See." Xander stuck his tongue out at his sister.

Eleni bustled down the stairs, her arms piled high with pie boxes. He hurried to take them from her.

"Oh, thank you. I have a few more in the house."

Dean carefully placed the pies in the back of his truck. "Do you have an old box? Something we can put these in, so they don't rattle around."

Eleni glanced toward the house, then back. "I have the big cooler. We might be able to fit two next to each other and stack them."

"I'll get it from the shed. I know where I put it Friday night. Are you sure Georgie doesn't want to come with us?"

Eleni waved him off. "She's been knitting up a storm lately. It doesn't get that cold here in the winter, but we do have a few chilly days in January and February. She wants the kids to have hats and scarves. I think she's making some for you, too."

As Dean retrieved the cooler, he thought about how long he'd be here. He'd narrowed down the search to a handful of people, but still didn't have any clue further than that. Truthfully, he wasn't in a big rush to find out. The holiday promotion had gone through without a hitch, so he might have to wait until Valentine's Day packages. Marketing would be working on those now in order to get advertisements out in time.

Of course, being able to run the company from his tiny apartment on the island had kept him from needing to run back home. He'd always been remote, but prior to this, he'd put in ten or twelve-hour days. Lately, he'd found, with enough delegating, he could get the same work done in just a few. Could he stay here on the island for a little longer? Really get to know the staff and help restructure the resort?

The idea of staying around here permanently entered his head as he watched Eleni carry more pies to the truck. Hoisting the cooler in his hands, he trotted over to the truck and placed it in. Once Eleni had the dozen pies inside, he wrapped a bungee cord around it, securing it to the side of the truck bed.

Luckily, the older model truck had a bench seat with three seat belts. "We'll need to double buckle the kids, but together they don't even weigh that of a grown adult."

"It's okay. Just for today and because we aren't going far." Eleni helped the kids with their seat belt, then buckled herself in the middle. When Dean got in, the fit was snug and cozy. Having Eleni's thigh pressed against his was nothing to complain about.

"Secondhand Antiques is just a short way past Nadine and Marek's house. That same beach road, before you reach the lighthouse."

"I drove by yesterday. Since I had the day off, I figured I'd explore the island a little."

Eleni sighed. "I'd love to get two days off in a row sometime."

"Don't you get vacation time?"

"I do, but I haven't taken any in years. I'm always worried some emergency will come up and I'll need the time. Luckily, the resort lets you roll over vacation time."

Dean wondered if maybe Eleni needed someone to push her to take some time off. The woman worked far too hard between her job and her family. Even today, which was supposed to be a fun family outing, she was delivering pies she'd probably slaved over once she'd gotten home from work yesterday.

"Up ahead. That big red barn behind the white farmhouse. That's Sandpiper Bed and Breakfast. Just pull off the road near the shell driveway next to the barn."

"Is that where the pies go?"

Eleni nodded as he parked the truck. The kids unbuckled and jumped out of the vehicle.

"You can look for pumpkins, but make sure not to bother other people," she called after them.

"Are they safe being on their own over there?" He pointed to the large yard. Wheelbarrows were loaded with pumpkins, and wooden crates were filled with gourds. More pumpkins, corn stalks, and other decorations littered the area, all lined with hay bales.

After releasing the cord for the cooler, Eleni glanced sideways at him. "You lived in a city, didn't you?"

"Yeah."

"Maybe in the summer, when we're in full tourist mode, I might keep a tighter rein on the twins, but now...they're fine."

"Let me get that cooler. It's heavy."

Her eyes twinkled. "That's why I brought you along, my friend."

As she showed him where to set the pies, Dean rolled that word *friend* over in his mind. Truthfully, he'd like to be more with Eleni. There was no way he'd ever become like his brother with a lady in every port. Not that Dean had lots of ports. He was a homebody through and through.

An older woman made her way to the doorway and greeted them. "Eleni, dear, you are so sweet to make these for us. I've had so many requests already. Kat told me you'd be bringing some today. I have a feeling they'll be gone by the time we close."

"I can make more for next weekend if you think they'll sell. I'll try to get them here earlier, so you can put them out on Saturday, too. Let me introduce you to my muscle today. Dean Peters. Haddie Marshall. This is Kat's grandmother."

"Nice to meet you, Mrs. Marshall."

Haddie waved her hands in the air like she was shooing a fly. "Oh, none of that. Everyone around here calls me Gran. Plain and simple."

"Gran. Nice place you've got here."

Eleni's smile grew huge. "You should see some of the antiques she's got inside the barn. If I was ever able to afford a larger house, I'd probably buy out the place."

As Gran meandered away, he asked Eleni, "You like antiques?" Most of the stuff in her house was a mishmash of different styles, but knowing what she'd been through, he figured what she had was what she could afford.

Eleni's shoulders rose and fell as a sigh escaped her mouth. "Mmhmm. I love antiques and the history behind them. Plus, they're just so beautiful."

Like her. He had a feeling Eleni didn't hear that enough. He'd have to tell her again when they weren't in a public place with the kids running all around. With a dog.

"Is that Boomer with Thea and Xander?"

Peeking over her shoulder, Eleni nodded. "Ben's over there helping Gran, and I'm sure Kat's inside the antique barn ringing up sales and helping customers. They'll be fine."

The teenager manning the stand with the other treats handed them each a cup of warm apple cider. Eleni cocked her head toward a low stack of hay bales. "Let's go sit for a few minutes while the kids get their energy out."

He followed her to two hay bales set aside from the others. Perching next to Eleni, he noticed more stacks of bales across the yard. The dog kept disappearing behind them.

"That's a small hay maze Ben created for the kids. It'll only last until the bales are all sold. He put these two aside for me, so I can decorate the house."

"You really get into this Halloween thing, huh?"

Eleni kept her gaze on Thea and Xander. "I've got two children. It's kind of a prerequisite. Didn't you do Halloween up big when you were a kid?"

"Maybe when I was younger, but after the accident, it was just too hard to get around door to door. The houses in our neighborhood were pretty spread out, and it was difficult walking for a few years."

She swiveled toward him and patted his knee. "You never did tell me what kind of accident it was. Is it something you don't like talking about?"

He shrugged. He hadn't spoken about it in a long time, but he didn't hang around people often and none of his employees would dare ask him. "It was a bike accident."

"Bicycle or motorcycle?"

"I was ten. Bicycle. An angry dog chased me and tried to bite me."

"Which is why Boomer makes you nervous."

"I won't lie. I'm not exactly comfortable around dogs. I suppose I should make it a point to get over that fear."

Her hand clenched on his thigh. "So you fell off the bike?"

"More like flew off the bike and tumbled down a rocky ravine. Tore open my leg, cut my face, fractured a number of bones. I was in the hospital for a month while they tried to repair everything. One of the fractures in my leg was so bad it caused that leg to be half an inch shorter than the other. It's why I limp."

The smile she flashed his way made him warmer than the cider he was drinking. "It doesn't detract from your ability to do your job. I've seen you do some stuff I know I wouldn't be able to do. Does it still hurt?"

"The leg itself doesn't hurt, but when I'm on my feet all day, the discrepancy in height can make my hip ache."

"And you haven't thought of getting a job where you can sit once in a while?"

"I like staying active." Surprisingly, he'd found that true. Being stagnant in his office all day wasn't healthy, even if he spent an hour in his home gym after. "I have a shoe lift the doctor gave me. I had to push aside my pride and actually wear it. It's been better since."

"That's good. Otherwise, you could get really grumpy."

He laughed. "Aren't I always grumpy?"

She pressed her face closer to his. "That's all an act, so people don't bother you while you're working. You can't fool me."

"I can't, huh?" If she only knew.

"What I don't understand is why a nice guy like you isn't married."

"Not many women want a guy with a limp and a scar."

"That's a cop out. You're still one of the most handsome men I've ever met, scars and all. I'm surprised you don't have women flinging themselves at you left and right."

"No flinging. Left, right, or center." Unless you counted the gold diggers. Staying out of the limelight helped to eliminate those. "Don't forget, I can't have kids."

"There are women who don't want kids. Or women who already have some, like me. I'm very happy with my two little rug rats. Did you want children?"

He stared off across the street to the ocean beyond. "I knew early on I couldn't have them, so I made myself believe I didn't want them."

"That's what turned you into a Scrooge. You didn't need any ghosts of Christmas past or future. You just needed to hang out with my brood."

He tipped his head next to hers, pressing their foreheads together. "I like your brood. I like you, Eleni."

He'd been dying to kiss her again since he'd done it Friday night. He wouldn't wait any longer. As his lips skimmed hers, shouts from across the yard interrupted them.

"Mom, I found the biggest pumpkin! We have to get it."

Eleni sighed. "Okay. Maybe I'm not always happy with my rug rats."

CHAPTER ELEVEN

*E*leni and Dean sprang apart as the twins rushed over and bounced up and down, waving their arms. Her kids must have kiss radar.

"It's over here. You need to come see," Thea yelled, her eyes wide.

Xander, not to be outdone by his sister, grabbed her hand and tugged. "We have to get it before someone else buys it!"

Dean sighed loudly, but his grin was mischievous. "Guess we need to take a look at this great pumpkin. If it's as good as they say, we might have to buy it."

He really was great with the kids. It was a shame he didn't have any of his own. Would he ever consider taking on someone else's? It was probably too soon to be thinking along those lines.

Thea led the way as Xander bubbled on about it. "It's huge and perfectly round, with almost no weird spots. Well, it has a few but not as many as some of the other big ones."

Dean tipped his head as he stared at her. "No weird spots? Sounds like we might have a winner."

The pumpkin was indeed huge. "I'm not sure we'll be able to get that in the car."

"Mom, that's why we brought Mr. Dean's truck," Xander whined.

Thea bobbed her head. "And he's super strong. He can get it in the back."

She had no doubt Dean was strong, but this was massive. Where had Haddie gotten it? "It's got to weigh close to a hundred pounds. That's very heavy."

Xander stared at the man, his face scrunched up. "Can you do it, Mr. Dean?"

"Hmm." Dean tapped his chin with his forefinger. "A hundred pounds, you say." He glanced at her, away, then back again.

In seconds, he scooped her off the ground and twirled in a circle. The kids danced and squealed as Eleni held on for dear life.

"What are you doing?"

After setting her back on her feet and holding her steady until her head stopped spinning, he grinned at the twins. "I reckon your mom weighs a little over a hundred pounds, and I can pick her up."

Laughing, she bit her lip. "Yeah, slightly over a hundred pounds." She'd never say how slight.

"Then, the pumpkin is doable. But it'll be the one for the porch."

Eleni glared at the large orange fruit and sized it up. "It may have to stay at the bottom of the stairs. I don't need the porch collapsing under the weight."

Dean waved at the kids. "You still each need a smaller pumpkin. Go find them."

"You have to be able to carry it yourself, Xander, Thea."

As the kids toddled off, Dean slung his arm over her shoulder. "I'd guess the weight is more around fifty pounds. Doubtful it'll break the porch. And once you carve it—"

"Oh, you don't carve pumpkins here until the day before or of Halloween. It's too warm, and they'll get mushy and completely cave in. Usually, we draw a face on it until the day, then we carve."

"Huh. I never thought of that. Good thing I didn't try and get my own pumpkin. I would have failed dismally."

Pressing herself against him, she said, "You're welcome to share our pumpkins."

Dean squinted down at her. "If I'm hauling that huge thing back to the house, I'd better be able to share it."

They both laughed, and Eleni didn't remember the last time she'd felt so light with someone other than the kids. The warmth from his body heated her up, and she wanted to kiss him again. Here, in a public venue, was hardly the place.

Gathering her courage, she took a chance and glanced up at him. "Once the pumpkins are back and the kids are busy, do you think you might like to take a walk to the beach?"

A smirk crossed his face. "Just you and me? Alone? With no chaperone?"

"That was kind of the point. I mean, we don't have to. We can just sit around with the kids and eat leftover pie."

Dean's eyes darted around, then he whispered in her ear. "As much as I love pie, I think I'd like you alone on a beach much better."

Eleni shivered at the words and the breath that brushed against her cheek. "If you're real nice, maybe I could arrange pie and then a walk."

The hand draped over her shoulder brushed along her skin, causing tingles wherever it touched. She'd never had such a desire to pull a man behind the barn and have her way with him in all her years. Especially since she'd had the twins. They were her life. Always. But right now, she wouldn't mind someone else being responsible for them for a while.

"Who do we see about this pumpkin and paying for it?"

Eleni twisted around, until she found Ben transferring corn stalks from a cart to lean against the side of the barn. She waved at him, and he sauntered over.

"Hey, Eleni, Dean. Good to see you again. You got something picked out?"

Dean pointed at the massive pumpkin. "The kids have their heart set on this monster."

Ben laughed, then glanced around the yard. "Can you back your vehicle up a bit closer? Between the two of us we should be able to set this baby inside."

"I'll get my truck. Eleni, why don't you find the kids and see what they chose for their individual pumpkins?"

As she maneuvered through the patch, she peeked back and noticed Dean handing some bills over to Ben. No, he didn't have to do that. She'd have to repay him once they got back. The kids had squatted next to the pumpkins they'd chosen.

"Can you carry them? Dean's driving the truck over to the big pumpkin. You only need to bring it that far."

Xander wiped his brow dramatically. "Phew. I wasn't sure if I was gonna make it to the road."

Eleni grinned at her little urchins as they hoisted their newfound gains and slogged behind her to the truck. Miraculously, the huge one had already been loaded.

"How did you get it up there?"

Ben pointed to two long planks of wood. "We rolled it halfway, then lifted the boards. Easy."

Eleni pursed her lips. "I think I have some wood somewhere in the back of the shed. It'll be easier to get down, right?"

Dean chuckled. "Gravity will take care of that, but we'll still need to make sure it doesn't go too fast or we'll be scraping pumpkin off the street for a week."

"Thanks, Ben. We've also got these two little ones, plus the hay bales, and I'd love to get a few corn stalks to tie to my lamp post. How much do I owe you?"

Ben waved his hand. "Dean gave me plenty, and the corn stalks are on us, since you brought us all the pies."

"But Haddie pays me for the pies once they've been sold. Fine. We'll call it even."

While she buckled the twins in the front, Dean and Ben tossed in the bales and stalks. She came around the front and was about to slide in the middle when Dean approached.

"I'll pay you back for the pumpkins. Let me know how much they were?"

Dean ran his hand up her arm, helping her get in. "Nope. It's my gift to the kids. If you pay me back, it makes my present null and void."

She wanted to argue, but it was a really sweet thing to do. He probably felt guilty that she'd been bringing him lunch every day and he'd been stopping by for dessert most nights. Guess she could deal with him paying for a few pumpkins.

As they drove back, the kids pointed out their favorite spots along the way. Dean seemed to take it all in stride and even asked them questions about what they liked to do best at these locations.

When they arrived at the house, he backed the truck as close to the porch as he could. The kids darted out and into the house to tell their grandmother about the monster pumpkin they'd found.

In minutes, they'd gotten the boards and rolled the large fruit to sit at the bottom of the stairs. Dean hefted the hay bales, corn stalks, and the two smaller pumpkins from the bed, then repositioned the vehicle on the street.

For the next half hour, the kids used markers to draw scary faces as she tied the stalks to her lamp posts. The hay bales were positioned on each side of the driveway, and she placed some potted mums on top of them.

Dean stayed for a light lunch of sandwiches, then the kids begged to watch a movie they'd been dying to see. She didn't like them glued to the tube all day, but for now, she'd agree.

When the twins were settled, her mom sat next to them and clicked on the closed captions. She'd wanted to see this movie, as well. While Eleni cleaned up the lunch dishes, Dean brought a few cups over to the sink. His breath on her neck chilled her.

"I believe you promised me a walk on the beach."

Swiveling in his arms, she started to reply, but his expression stopped her. The look in his eyes promised more than a walk.

Dean inhaled the tempting aroma that was Eleni. She spun in his arms and gazed into his eyes. What did she see? Still a poor man who cleaned up trash and swept floors, or did she see who he really was? Not the rich business owner. The man who was starting to have strong feelings for her, something he'd never allowed with any other woman.

"I'd love a walk along the beach. Let me tell Mom where we're going first."

She scurried off and returned a few moments later with a fleece. "It can get cool by the ocean at times. Do you need something? I might have an old sweatshirt of Sean's."

"My coat is in the truck. I'll grab it on the way."

They crept out the back so as not to distract the kids. After retrieving and putting on his denim coat, he took Eleni's hand and held his other out in front. "What's the best beach to go to from here?"

"The best one is up by the lighthouse and would take us an hour to walk there. We can go to the one by The Sands. It's closer and has great views."

"I kind of like the views from here." He tugged on her hand to draw her nearer.

"There you go flattering me again. We ate all the pie. You'll have to wait until I bake again."

Dean wanted to tell her he didn't care about the pie or any of the food she made. The biggest draw for him to visit was her. The kids and her mom came in a close second.

"Have you lived on the island long?" It was time to get to know her a little better. Not because he suspected her of subterfuge at The Pearl. The more time he spent in her presence, the more she intrigued him, and he wanted to know everything about Eleni Griffin.

"About sixteen years."

He paused in his step. "Wow. How old were you when you moved here?"

She crossed her arms and started walking again. "Is that a roundabout way of asking how old I am?"

He shook his head and grinned. "No, sorry. I guess I assumed you'd moved here with your husband."

"I grew up in Summerville, just off-island, and visited often. When I was twenty-one, some friends and I rented a place and got summer jobs here. Two of us decided to stay and work year-round."

"Did you work at The Pearl?" He knew she hadn't. Why was he asking?

"I worked at a lot of places. Did a bunch of waitressing at Rods and J Roger. Was grounds crew at the campground. Even worked the information desk at the Welcome Center for a while."

"Which did you like the best?"

Eleni bit her lip and glanced away. "I was young and looking for some fun, so any place that had cute guys, which wasn't the Welcome Center. That's where lots of older people and families stop. Occasionally, you'd get a group of guys at the campground, but mostly they were too cheap to take you out or do anything. Waitressing was good for connecting with people and the tips were great."

"I'll bet you got lots of tips. With your sunshine personality, you'd have done well."

Her cheeks got pink, and she stared at her feet for a second. "Thanks. It was fun."

"Is that where you met your husband?" Did she not like to talk about the man? Was he bringing up a sore subject?

"He was doing some electrical work on the Ferry Boat dock. My friends and I liked to hang around the pier right next to it to check out who was getting off the ferry. We got to know each other and ended up dating, then getting married.

"When did you end up at The Pearl?"

"Money got tight after the twins were born. I wasn't working any longer, and the expenses were tough. Plus, as I'm sure you've seen, anything you buy on the island costs more than if you go to the mainland. With two babies, I rarely had an opportunity to do my shopping there. I started at The Pearl on the registration desk, because I could work nights and Sean was home with the kids. I worked my way up to Administrative Assistant. A lot of the other places here won't give you full-time hours in the off season. I took what I could get."

"Do you like your job?"

"I do. Hugh can be a...well, you've met the man. I'm sure I don't need to explain. But I love working for Aarya, and so many of the other staff are wonderful and friendly."

Yeah, that Hugh thing would need to be addressed. Dean's thoughts on the man weren't quite so tactful.

The beach came into view and the resort, The Sands, next to it. Dean gave her a hip bump and smirked. "Are we allowed to be this close to the competition?"

Eleni's gorgeous laugh filled the air. "I think it's permitted. I come here all the time. I've got friends who work at the hotel."

"In administration like you?" Had Eleni inadvertently given away some of their marketing without even knowing it? No way she'd do it purposely.

"No. A few work in housekeeping and one runs the chair rentals on the beach in the summer. In the winter, she heads farther south. She's a total beach bum."

As he viewed the ocean waves rising and crashing, he said, "I can see why. It's so peaceful here."

"I love it. I can't imagine a scenario where I'd ever want to leave."

They strolled along the beach on the damp sand, out of the path of the waves. There were people here and there, walking dogs, playing Frisbee, reading books, but only a few brave souls dared to go in the water.

"Did your mom move here after your husband passed away?"

"She moved here permanently then, but she'd been staying over now and again when I needed help with the kids. When she started losing her hearing, it was a two-way street. She needed us. We needed her. My brother was deployed at that time, so she didn't have anyone else. My dad passed away about ten years ago."

"You have a brother in the military? I think Xander has mentioned him."

"Yup, Thaddeus. He was an oops when I was about ten. He's got another few years to serve, then I'm hoping to talk him into moving to the island with us."

Dean thought about his brother and wondered what it would be like to be near him for long periods of time. Assuming he could ever get his brother to stay in one place long enough. Trey was great at his job, but he loved the travel, the variety of women, and being able to get up and be somewhere else tomorrow. Not the kind of life Dean had ever wanted.

They took their time wandering the beach, with Eleni picking up pretty shells she thought the kids might like.

"They don't get sick of shells having lived their entire life on an island?"

Eleni gave him a look. "You can never get sick of looking for shells. If you don't understand that, we can't be friends."

Dragging her closer, he cupped her face. "What if I want to be more than friends with you?"

Her lips curled up, and she inhaled deeply. "I guess that was part of the reason for the walk. I was enjoying myself simply being with you. You're easy to talk to Dean Peters."

"I like listening to the sound of your voice, Eleni Griffin. Can we sit for a few minutes?"

"Oh, is your hip bothering you? I'm sorry. We didn't have to walk this far."

"I'm fine. I was kind of hoping it would be a little cooler out here, so I'd have to wrap you in my arms."

Her eyes gleamed. "I can pretend it's chilly. Ooh, ooh, that wind is really kicking up today. I should have brought something warmer to wear."

God, she was precious. He steered her toward a large outcropping of rock and sat with his back against one. Patting the sand in front of him, he cocked his head. "Right here. Warmest place around."

In seconds, his arms had encircled her, and she rested her back against his chest. A humming sound drifted toward him. "Mm, this is wonderful. So warm."

"Is there any way to get the temperature even higher?" Sweeping her hair off her neck, he placed his lips on her soft skin and pressed tiny kisses there.

She shivered, and Dean wanted to shout with success. Silly really, since he'd pleased women in the past. For some reason, making Eleni tremble ranked much higher than anything else he'd ever done.

Continuing on, he nibbled on her ear and inhaled her sweet fragrance. "If I had known this was my reward, I would have hefted a few dozen pumpkins for you months ago."

"Oh, God, you don't have to heft anything to do this. It's my absolute pleasure. I can't tell you how long it's been since a man nibbled on my neck."

"The men around here are stupid, then. I know a good thing when I see it."

Eleni tilted her head, and Dean chuckled at her subtle hint. He didn't need to be told twice. He glided his mouth along her jawline, across her cheeks, kissed the tip of her nose, then skimmed under her eyes back to her ear. Her head settled on his shoulder, and he shifted so they faced each other a little more.

"I can't get those kisses we shared a few days ago out of my mind."

Eleni's eyes opened and stared dreamily at the sky. "They were very nice."

"Only nice? Ouch. I think I need to up my game if all I'm getting ranked is nice."

She wrinkled her nose. "I said *very* nice."

"Still. I like to be at the top of my field. I'll have to experiment some to see how I can improve."

Dean spent the next half hour doing just that.

CHAPTER TWELVE

"I can't believe you haven't found the culprit yet."

Dean listened as Trey went on and on about his inability to discover who was leaking information.

"It hasn't happened again. It's not easy to find who's giving away secrets when they aren't currently doing it. Are you sure we haven't somehow tipped them off that I'm here?"

Trey snorted. "I haven't even told anyone. You never come into the office, anyway, so who would know that you aren't at your house?"

"No one except Maggie. I seriously doubt she's giving away marketing secrets. The Ocean Pearl is the only resort it's happened to. The leak is most likely here. If I can run the company remotely, then it doesn't matter when I come back, does it?"

Dean hated the idea of going back to his sterile house, where he lived by himself. Sure, he had a cleaning lady twice a week. His assistant was there during the workdays, but she had her own office and only bothered him if there was something she couldn't do. Which was very little. He had a cook who made his meals three times a week and left them in the fridge for him with detailed instructions on heating.

There were never brownies or apple pie for dessert. No basketball, walks on the beach, or pumpkin decorating.

"I'm surprised you aren't screaming to come back." Trey's voice shifted his attention back to the phone. "You like cleaning toilets and emptying trash all of a sudden?"

"The people who do this ought to get a huge raise. You should see some of the stuff I've had to deal with."

"Ah, no thanks, brother. I'm happy paying for someone else to do that. So, what's really keeping you on the island? You taking advantage of the island babes? I never even gave you my list."

Trey and his beach babes. "I don't need your list."

"Oh, you found some on your own. Do tell. I may need you to share your list for the next time I visit."

Like that would ever happen. Eleni was Dean's. For now. After their little make out session on the beach a few days ago, he wanted to claim her and mark her as taken. Caveman much?

"It's not what you think. I gotta go."

"Why? Where are you going?"

"Trick or Treating. It's Halloween."

Trey laughed. "Really? What are you wearing for a costume?"

Dean stayed silent as he looked down at his cowboy boots. His brother wouldn't understand.

"Oh, my God. Are you seriously wearing a costume? What? You have to tell me."

Dean sighed. "It's nothing major. A few of us are wearing cowboy hats and boots with long duster jackets or leather vests."

"Us? Who's this us?"

"Believe it or not, I have made some friends while I've been here."

"Female friends?"

Dean shook his head at his brother's reply. He never changed. "Some of them are female and some are male. It's just a big group of people. The town has a parade down Main Street with a bunch of stuff for the kids to do."

"And you're hanging around with people who have kids?"

Yeah, Trey was one of the only people who knew his secret. Trey and Eleni.

"There are kids on the island."

"I may have to come visit and check out what's happened to my big brother."

"No, don't. We don't want anyone catching us together. We may not look exactly alike, but standing side by side, someone might notice the similarities. I'll call you later. I gotta go." Dean disconnected the call and shoved the phone in his pocket. He was almost at Eleni's.

Thea and Xander had been hyper lately, with all the excitement about their costumes and the Main Street parade. Marek and Nadine had talked him and Eleni into dressing up in a group costume and reenacting the Gunfight at the OK Corral. They'd spent time last weekend all watching the movie while the kids had a sleepover. Dean didn't ever remember doing anything similar in his life. Now, he didn't know why he hadn't. These people were fun to be around.

As he rounded the corner, kids' happy screams could be heard coming from the yard. Xander zoomed into the street, then screeched as he spun and rocketed back toward the house.

"I thought you were an astronaut, not a race car," Dean called out to the boy in the white jumpsuit, wearing a space helmet made from a gallon milk jug.

"I am. But astronauts blast into space in their spaceships, so I need to go fast."

"Look at me, Mr. Dean." Thea romped toward him, her brown hair in two ponytails, hanging like doggy ears on the side of her head. Her nose was painted black, and she had a white spot colored in around one eye. Her one-piece costume was black with large white spots. A twin to Cuddles, her stuffed puppy.

Livy pranced around in a similar fuzzy, one-piece outfit. This one was light pink, and she wore a hood with a unicorn horn.

Kandra had everyone beat, at least in Dean's mind. She wore a baggy, blue jumpsuit, a helmet, and goggles. Strapped to her back was a backpack and above her head were two stiff ropes with a tiny parachute attached.

"How did you get that to stay up there?" Dean asked Marek as he joined the adults.

The man smoothed down his fake handlebar mustache and smirked. "I stuffed some dowels inside the rope. I'm hoping she'll get a prize for it."

Nadine rolled her eyes. "I think he's more excited about the costume contest than the kids are. They just like dressing up."

"Well, howdy, partner." Eleni swaggered over, her cowboy hat low over her face. She wore a long dark coat, with a bolo tie and cowboy boots. A badge was pinned to the lapel.

"Sheriff. What kind of trouble are we expecting today?"

"Seems Ike Clanton and some of his boys plan to be in town today. I could use a little back up."

Nadine and Marek laughed, then slapped their cowboy hats on their heads.

"Guess we better saddle up if we want to get these desperadoes to town on time." Nadine called out to the kids, who all ran towards them with little pumpkin buckets in their hands.

"Is Georgie coming with us?" Dean asked Eleni.

A sly smile crept onto her face. "Vlad picked her up an hour ago. Said he needed her cooking expertise for some of the goodies they'll give to the kids after the parade."

Dean was happy for the woman. She definitely was a prize. Vlad was also one of the staff members he enjoyed being around. The man was as nice as he was talented in the kitchen.

"Head 'em up and move 'em out," Marek yelled to the kids, and they all fell into step ahead of the adults.

Once they were on the road, Dean sidled closer to Eleni and snagged her hand. He'd wanted to give her a big kiss as soon as he'd seen her today, but what they had was still too new. It was ridiculous he even thought that. How many women had he slept with who he'd only known for a few hours? Not as many as Trey obviously, but still it was more his way of hooking up. Long term had never been his goal. With Eleni, he couldn't see any other way.

So what happens when you leave here?

He hated that question. At some point, the truth would come out and then what? *You could tell her the truth now.*

Sure, and have her hate him before he could get her to really know him, know him as something more than a wealthy businessman. He'd had too many women play up to him simply because of his money. Eleni wasn't a gold digger, but he never wanted her to be swayed into seeing him because he could provide for her and the kids. He had to know it was Dean she liked and wanted to be with. So far it was.

"So are there any places downtown where we could sneak off and do a little smooching?" He wiggled his eyebrows up and down.

Eleni hung onto his arm and laughed. "You're so cute. Maybe after we come back and get the kids settled. If my mother makes it back, too, we could take another walk."

"I did enjoy our beach walk the other day." Dean tilted her hat back, then removed his and held it in front of their faces. He pressed a kiss to her sweet lips quickly, then slapped his hat back on his head. "That'll have to do for now."

Downtown was decorated with hay bales, pumpkins, fall flowers, and cornstalks tied to every post and pole. Shop keepers stood on their stoops with bags of candy and goodies, waiting to fill the empty buckets of the local children.

The mayor, dressed in an old-time outfit, stood at the end of Main Street where the businesses started. She spread the children out in pairs, then waved the golf cart in front of her to start. Music blared from the speakers as she led the parade.

As the kids passed each business, they darted from side to side, gathering their spoils.

"Do we join in or stay to the side?" Dean had never seen something like this before.

"We can do either. My kids are old enough that they don't need me holding their hand anymore. When they were really small, I walked with them."

The costumes ranged from store bought to handmade, simple to outlandish. There was a child being pushed in a wheelchair that had a spaceship surrounding her.

"That's incredible. What a great idea."

"That's Robyn. Her dad builds a unique costume to go with her wheelchair every year. The man is super creative and loves his daughter. He wants her to be able to participate in the town event, as well."

Dean wondered what he would have been like if he'd had the opportunity to have children. Especially a child with special needs. Would he have been overwhelmed or risen to the challenge like this man? He liked to think he'd be the latter.

Main Street wasn't that long, so the parade ended quickly enough. Songs like "The Monster Mash" and "Thriller" blared from speakers, and once they reached the town common, the kids spread out and danced to the tunes.

Marek and Nadine jumped in with their kids doing some strange dance where they looked like monsters, and Dean only shook his head when they signaled for him to join them.

He waved Eleni on. "You can go if you want, but I haven't got a clue what they're doing."

She hung on his arm and laughed. The sound was so sweet. "That's okay. I love simply watching them have fun."

A few songs later, the music was turned off, and the mayor waved for people to quiet down.

"We've got the results of the costume contest. As you know, several islanders are chosen each year to be anonymous judges and pick winners in a number of categories."

The kids all held their breath as winners and runners up were announced.

"They've got a lot of categories, huh?"

Eleni's smile was brighter than the sun. "That's why I love this place. They try and give prizes to most of the kids if they can. They pick overall best for lots of different age groups, but each year they make up new awards to fit some of the costumes, so everyone gets something."

Xander rushed over with his Out of This World prize. Thea had Cuddliest award. Livy had Most Magical costume, and Kandra had a smug look with hers. Up, Up, and Away the Best.

Dean had to wonder, when his dad had chosen Last Chance Beach for a resort, had he known about the magic of this island? About the incredible people who lived here? Trey had never mentioned anything beyond sun, sand, and surf. Well, the beach babes had ranked up high for him, too.

"What do we do now?"

Eleni waved her hand to the end building. A small shop had picnic tables spread around a grassy area next to it. A line had formed at a window on the side.

"The bakery gives out free hot chocolate or mulled cider."

"Thea and Xander are already queued up. Should we get in line or is it only for the kids?"

When Marek and Nadine scooted over, he had his answer.

Eleni tugged on his arm. "We should get some. Vlad makes the mulled cider, and it's so good."

As they ambled over to stand in line, Dean realized there was a lot about this island that was good.

CHAPTER THIRTEEN

*E*leni washed the last dish and handed it to Dean, who was drying. She'd finally gotten him to come over for Sunday dinner. At first, she'd been nervous that what she made wouldn't be good enough, but he ate her cooking every day when she brought it for lunch and had never complained.

"You're spoiling me, Leni. I'll need to walk around the island a few times every night, so I don't need to let out another notch on my belt."

She threw him a side eye. "There's nothing wrong with where your belt is or the waist it's on."

She slid her arms around said waist and rested on his chest. It was lovely how he immediately pulled her close and pressed a kiss to her hair. The kisses he shared with her lips weren't bad either. With the kids around, it didn't happen as often as she'd like.

"I promised Thea and Xander I'd take them to the lighthouse today and then to Sandpiper Point to look for shells. They always find really great ones there. Did you want to come?"

"Sounds like a nice day."

Eleni pressed her lips together and looked away. Dean touched her shoulders and tipped his head down to hers.

"What's wrong? Do you not want me to come?"

"Oh, no, it's not that. Of course, we want you with us. We thought we'd ride the bikes there. Now that it's November, the traffic on the beach roads has dwindled and it's much safer."

"Bikes?" His face tightened at the word.

Patting his arm, she shook her head. "If you want to meet us there, we could do that. I know you aren't crazy about riding bikes."

Dean's breath went in and out slowly. "I don't like bikes. Haven't ridden one in over thirty years, but I don't want to keep the kids from having their fun day."

"Follow us in the truck. It'll be fine."

Eleni could see a war battling in Dean's eyes. What in the world was going on inside his head?

His brows came together. "I was just telling Xander the other day that it isn't good to give in to fear. That you have to face your demons in order to win over them."

"You were talking about his math test, not getting on something that caused you lots of pain in the past."

"It doesn't matter what it is. Or it shouldn't. I've been a coward for too many years and never faced this demon. Maybe it's time I do." His face was set in stone.

"Are you sure?"

His eyes rose to the ceiling. "I am, but I don't actually have a bike to use."

"I still have Sean's bike. I kept it as a spare for when we needed an extra. Like now. My mother uses it occasionally. Did you want to use it? You really don't have to."

Dean glanced around the kitchen and cocked his head when he heard the kids talking in the living room. A determined look came onto his face, and he gave a quick nod. "Do you think I could try it first before the kids come outside? It's been a long time."

Eleni hugged him tightly and said, "Of course. I just filled the tires when I did the other bikes last week. Let's sneak out now while they're occupied."

The bike was in the shed behind hers and the kids', but they all needed to come out, anyway. Dean stared at the bicycle like it was a dragon ready to eat him alive. After a few cleansing breaths, he rolled it to the street and mounted. She handed him a helmet, and he adjusted it, then clicked the connection. He gripped the handlebars until his knuckles were white, but he pushed off, and after a few wobbles, rode down the street.

When he'd gotten three houses down, he turned perfectly and pedaled back. His face showed his triumph.

She ran up to him as soon as he stopped, cupped his face, and kissed him. "You were amazing."

"I guess I didn't forget."

Shrugging, she said, "It's like riding a bike."

Dean slapped his forehead with his palm and groaned. "Better get the kids out here before any other bad jokes start flying. I'll practice a bit more."

She ran back into the house and shouted for them to fall out, then she stuffed the food she'd prepared earlier into her backpack. By the time she got outside, Thea and Xander had already gotten on their bikes with their helmets and were cruising up and down the street with Dean.

Soon, she joined them. "Turn at the Fire Department. We'll take Windsurfer Ave. to the lighthouse."

The kids rode on ahead, and Eleni pulled up adjacent to Dean. It was nice with less traffic this time of year, yet the weather was still warm and the sun shone bright.

"Are you okay?" She studied Dean's face, looking for any signs of anxiety. His jaw was tense but other than that, he didn't seem overly worried.

"This is kind of fun. I've forgotten what it was like to ride a bike. My leg was a mess for so long as a kid that I never dared get back on. As I got older, my mode of transportation was more along the lines of four wheels. I don't think it ever occurred to me to get back on a bike again."

"And you're not in any pain?" She worried about how it would affect his hip and leg.

His lips twisted up on one side. "Feels great. I may have another opinion after a day on this, but for now, it's all good."

Even though Dean said he was fine, Eleni still kept her eyes on him as they rode. They caught up to the kids as they parked their bikes at the lighthouse. A few cars dotted the parking lot, but it was relatively empty.

"Do you have a lock for them?" Dean asked, studying the area.

"We won't need it. In the summer, maybe, but at this time of year, I doubt anything would happen to the bikes."

He looked hesitant, but left the bike next to the others, his helmet hanging off the handlebars like the others.

"Mr. Dean, are you gonna walk to the top with us?" Xander bounced in front of them, his expression hopeful. Eleni wished he had more of a man's presence around as a role model. Whenever Dean came over, Xander wanted to be with him every second. She understood, because she'd begun to feel the same way.

"Is it going to be too hard for me?"

Xander shook his head. "Nah, mom can do it, and she's almost as old as you."

Eleni swatted at her son, but he ducked away before she could reach him. Waggling her finger at him, she warned, "For that, you'll be on trash duty for the next week."

Her son laughed and drew on Dean's hand to head inside. Between both kids, Dean got a lesson on the history of the lighthouse and how each lighthouse was different to help boats navigate and know where they were. Pride rushed in that they'd remembered the lessons she'd taught them.

"Wow, you two are very knowledgeable about this place. Can you give me a tour?"

Eleni followed behind as they climbed up the narrow winding staircase. Every now and then Dean's gait was off, and he held tighter to the railing, but the chatting he and the kids were doing never paused.

At the top, they viewed the scenery in every direction.

"Wow. It's gorgeous from up here." Dean sidled up next to her and finagled his fingers into hers. Thea and Xander wandered a few feet away. Lifting his face up, he sniffed a few times. "Smells like a cigar. People just don't follow rules anymore. There's a no smoking sign at the bottom of the stairs."

Eleni grinned and pressed closer. "That's probably Cornelius Wiley. He was the lighthouse keeper back in the late 1800s."

Dean's eyes narrowed, and his lips pressed together. "You're serious?"

"There's a rumor the place is haunted. People smell his cigar all the time. Some have even seen him up here on foggy nights. I haven't mentioned it in the lessons to the kids, because I wasn't sure how they'd react. They're still young, and I didn't want to scare them. They love coming up here."

His mouth touched her ear. "Are you scared?"

She gazed up at him with a smile. "What would you do if I was?"

"I might have to protect you, keep you safe and comforted." His arm draped across her shoulder, and she snuggled in closer.

When was the last time someone had comforted her? Her mother and kids were always around, but typically she was the one doing the comforting, never on the receiving end.

They took another ten minutes up the top, and the kids took turns pointing out places in the distance. Unfortunately, Dean had to remove his arm when they climbed back down.

"Mom, did you bring food so we can eat on the beach?" Thea yelled as she pranced over to the picnic tables on the edge of the sand.

"I did. It's in my bag on the bike. You and your brother can go get it and bring it back here."

When the kids looked to complain, she gave them the mom look and they rushed off.

"You do that very well. I remember my mother had it down pat. My brother and I practically quaked in our boots if she threw it at us."

"What's your brother do?"

Dean stared off at the ocean waves rolling in. "He's in finance."

"Does he live on Cape Cod?"

Shaking his head, Dean said, "He travels a good deal with his job, but his home base is Boston."

"Did you see him much when you lived there?"

"When he was in the area, sure. But I'm a homebody, and he's a bit of a party boy. Maybe someday he'll settle down."

"Like you?" The kids ran back and plopped the bag on the table. Dean pushed it in front of her to open.

It wasn't until she'd distributed the food and they had eaten half of it that he answered her question.

"I always thought I liked being by myself and was happy the way my life was. These last few months have shown me a very different lifestyle."

Reaching over, she grasped his hand. "Different, but not bad?"

"Definitely not bad. I hadn't realized what I'd been missing. Thanks for dragging me out of my solitary rut, even if it was kicking and screaming."

"You didn't kick at all, and the screaming wasn't very loud."

Thea tipped her head at their conversation. "What were you screaming about?"

They both laughed, and Dean squeezed her hand. Once they finished their lunch and cleaned it up, the kids jumped all over the place.

"They've got the best shells on this beach, Mr. Dean." Thea yanked at his hand until they all traipsed down the dune to the sand.

Xander and Thea raced back and forth, showing off their shiny treasures and frolicking as the waves chased them up the beach. When they got farther away from the lighthouse, Xander waved his arms and trotted over.

"Mom, that house we love is still for sale. Mr. Dean, Mom's going to buy that for us."

Eleni stared past the sea grass at an adorable cottage tucked privately back from the beach. Aptly named The Hideaway.

"In your dreams, sweetie."

Dean followed the direction of Xander's hand. "I didn't even realize there was a house back there."

Thea stumbled over and fell on the sand near them. "I love that house. Mom, we need to get it, so we all have a bedroom."

Dean cocked his head and studied the cottage. "Are you looking to buy another house? Yours is in a great neighborhood, unless you want to be on the ocean."

"My house is fine for now, but Xander and Thea share a bedroom. In another few years, that won't be too cool. Not sure what I'll do then. Maybe give one of them my room, and I can sleep on the pull-out couch in the living room."

Dean lifted one eyebrow at her.

As the twins darted away again to find shells, Eleni grinned. "It'll come in handy when they're teenagers, and they try and sneak in the house after curfew. That house is nice and private and has four bedrooms. Plenty of room for all of us."

"It looks like it needs some work. You might be able to get it for a good deal."

"Sure, it's priced lower than some of the others on the island that are renovated, but since it's on the beach, it's still way out of my price range."

She gave a big sigh, then spun to locate the kids.

"Have you been inside it? It could be horrible."

"Yeah. Years ago, when I first came to the island, I got a peek inside. It's perfect. What they call great bones. And being here on the ocean would be wonderful for mom. She used to love listening to the sound of the waves, but at least she'd be able to see them rolling and crashing."

Dean examined it again, his mouth turning down. "Lots of work to do."

Curling her hand through his arm, she said, "It simply needs love and a good family to live in it. Nothing else is important.

CHAPTER FOURTEEN

*D*ean gazed at Eleni's face as she took in the weather-worn house. The difference in mindsets between her and most of the women he'd known was night and day. Instead of wanting room service and all the amenities a five-star resort could offer, Eleni would be happy cleaning up an old cottage, simply because it gave her children more room and her mom a lovely view now that her sense of hearing no longer worked.

Giving. The word described Eleni perfectly. Right down to making sure he wasn't uncomfortable riding the bike here today. She'd given him plenty of opportunities to join them in their day trip, using his truck instead.

No one was more surprised than him when he'd gotten on that bike and successfully pedaled it down the street. He'd never tell her the panic that had welled up inside or the memories that had surfaced of him crashing and falling. But he'd done it, and damn, it felt amazing. Like he'd climbed to the top of the highest mountain.

The kids scampered from the waves up to where the sea grass started, their eyes intent on finding the best shells. Xander plunked down on the line where the beach went from damp to dry and started wiggling his finger in the sand.

"Mom, come here and see this."

Eleni gave a sweet laugh and jogged off toward her son as Thea sprinted toward him, her hand held out.

"Look at this one, Mr. Dean. What do you think?"

He gazed at the shiny shell. "It's pretty, but not as pretty as you."

Thea giggled, then her lips thinned, and she stared at him solemnly. "Mr. Dean?"

He couldn't wait for her question. She always had such unique conversations with him. Strange how he never knew what fascinating beings small children were.

"Do you like Mom?"

Okay, that wasn't what he was expecting. "Of course, I like her. Your mom is a nice lady."

The girl nibbled on her lip, then scrunched up her nose. "I mean...you hold her hand. A lot."

Dean breathed out in relief that the only thing she'd seen was the hand holding. "I don't want her to get lost."

Thea rolled her eyes as well as any adult he'd seen. "She's lived on this island a long time. I doubt she'd get lost."

"Well, maybe *I* don't want to get lost. I haven't been here that long."

Her tiny face was so adorable when she was thinking. Sidling closer, she wedged her hand into his. It was such a rare feeling. Not unpleasant at all and maybe even a little comforting.

Her chin tipped up, and her brows drew together. "Do you want to be boyfriends with Mom? She's never had one before."

Oh, man. What did he say to that? He'd love to be way more than boyfriends with her mom. Not something an eight-year-old needed to know.

"Well, I think she loved your dad a lot, and it's hard for her to think of someone else that way."

Thea nodded slowly, thoughtfully. "Yeah, I think so, too. But I think it's also hard because she has to take care of Xander and me and Yia Yia. Even though Yia Yia helps watch us, she still can't do some things, like lift heavy pumpkins."

As Thea twisted to check where her mother was, she tightened her grip on his hand. He squeezed back to let her know he was here for her.

When Thea jerked on his hand, he bent down close to her face as she said in a soft voice, "I think Mom could use a boyfriend. Do you think you could be her boyfriend?"

He pursed his lips and closed one eye. "I don't know. What do I have to do?"

Let's hope she didn't know exactly what the job entailed.

Her tongue poked out of her mouth and slid to the side. "Uh, hold her hand. Make her laugh."

"Okay. I do some of that now, don't I?"

"Hmm. Yeah, you do. But I think when you're her boyfriend, you might have to kiss her."

He reared back and made a terrified face. "Really?"

Thea's eyes opened wide, and she tugged again. "It's not so bad. Mom smells really good, and her skin is so soft. You should touch it and see."

Oh, this little girl didn't know what she was asking. He was quite aware how soft Eleni's skin was and how intoxicating her fragrance was. It about knocked him off his feet every time he got close to her.

"Do you think your mom would want me to kiss her?" Put that ball back in her court.

Thea sucked her lip in, her gaze high in thought. "I think she'd like it. She says you're a nice man and very handsome."

"She told you that?"

"No, I heard Yia Yia say it to her, and Mom agreed. She likes watching you when you work at The Pearl. She said you have nice muscles."

Dean pushed back the chuckle that threatened to escape. Talk about little ears and what they heard. He needed to ask the tough question, though.

"Would you be okay if I was your mom's boyfriend? And how about Xander?"

"Oh, yeah. You're lots of fun." No hesitation. That was a good sign. "I like having you around, and Xander says he wishes you could come stay with us all the time, so he'd have another guy in the house. He doesn't complain too much, but I know sometimes he doesn't like all the girly stuff we do."

"I can't say I blame him. Although when he gets a little older, I'll bet he doesn't mind quite so much. Being with girls. Not necessarily doing the girly stuff."

"So, you'll do it? Be Mom's boyfriend?" The hopeful expression on her face made him want to give her everything.

"I think you're missing the most important part of this question. Does your mom want me to be her boyfriend?" God, what an old-fashioned term at his age.

"Mom!" Thea yelled, and Eleni came trotting over.

"Did you find a good shell?" Her gorgeous smile was in place. Would it stay there after her daughter got through?

"Mr. Dean and I were talking. I think he needs to be your boyfriend. 'Cause you don't have one and you need one."

Eleni's face stiffened, and she tilted her head. "Why do I need one?"

"So you can have another grownup to play with. Yia Yia is too old for you, and Nadine is married to Marek, and Mr. Dean really likes you. He says you're a nice lady."

"He does, does he?" Eleni pinned him with her gaze.

Dean took Eleni's hand and drew her near. "Yes, he does. Thea brought it up, but I have to admit I kind of like the idea. That is, if you're okay with it?"

Her lips twitched. "You want to be my boyfriend?"

He shrugged, his own grin popping out. "I'm not opposed to the idea. Only if it's something you want."

"I suppose we could try it. Would we go on a date?" She wiggled her eyebrows.

Dean bent down to Thea and mock whispered, "Do we go on dates if I'm her boyfriend?"

Thea's head bobbed up and down rapidly. "You can take her to a fancy restaurant and buy her flowers and candy."

"I think I could do that." He straightened up and asked, "Eleni, would you like to go to a fancy restaurant with me?"

She paused. Did she not want to go out with him?

"I would, but it doesn't have to be any place real expensive. A cup of coffee at Playing Hookey would be okay, too."

Ah, she didn't want him spending too much money on her. If only she knew. Boy, was it refreshing to find a woman who didn't want everything she could get. Who actually considered what he could afford.

"I've got a little saved up for a rainy day. I think we could splurge."

"Then, I guess a date would be nice. Is that okay with you, Thea, my little matchmaker?"

The girl crossed her arms over her chest and nodded. "Yeah, but maybe you should try the kissing first just to make sure it's okay. Mr. Dean was worried about that."

Eleni's eyes gleamed. "You were worried about the kiss? Did you think it wouldn't be good?" The challenge in her stare sucker punched him. This woman was something.

"I wasn't certain, but Thea assured me you smell good and your skin is soft. It should be okay."

Thea waved her hand between them. "Go ahead and try it, Mom. I'm gonna go show Xander my shell."

As the girl ran off, Eleni doubled over laughing. Dean caught her and joined in. For a few moments, they enjoyed holding each other and watching the kids.

"I'm so sorry Thea cornered you like that. She's getting to be quite a handful."

Dean caressed her face, then tipped her chin toward him. "I'm not sorry at all. It makes it okay to do this." When his lips touched hers, he readily conceded that she smelled good, and her skin was quite soft.

Eleni rushed into the living room and addressed her family. "Has anyone seen my hairbrush? Dean will be picking me up in ten minutes, and I've got a rat's nest on my head." There hadn't been time to wash her hair in the shower when she'd gotten home, plus dry and style it.

Xander pointed at his sister, who was sitting on the floor. As she stepped closer, Eleni wanted to cry. Thea was combing Cuddles' fur with her good brush. The girl looked up, sheepish expression firmly in place.

"This boyfriend date thing was your idea, little lady. What will Dean think when he picks me up and I look like I've been standing in a gale force wind for an hour?"

Thea jumped to her feet and wrapped her arms around Eleni's legs. God, she hated when they did that because it took away the mad.

"He'll think you're beautiful, Mom. Because you are. Look at this pretty dress. It has teeny, little flowers all over it, and you smell so good." The child took an exaggerated sniff and pretended to swoon. Where did she get the dramatics from? Certainly not her.

Taking the brush, Eleni instructed, "If Dean gets here before I'm ready, it's your job to keep him occupied until I am. Got it?"

"Yup." Thea hopped to the front window and sat with her head in her hands, watching.

Scooting back down the hallway, Eleni got her hair under control, then touched up her make-up. She rarely wore tons, but tonight she'd decided on some smoky eye shadow and a little more mascara than usual. She stroked on a soft pink lipstick, then slipped on her nice shoes. It wasn't often she wore heels this high. At work, they'd hurt her feet if she had to run around the building too much. Tonight was the perfect time to wear them.

A commotion in the living room drifted down the hall, and she peeked out of her room. Dean stood with the kids and her mom, and Eleni's breath caught. Wow. She'd thought he looked good in his work outfit or in his jeans and t-shirts, but this...

He wore a black suit, white shirt, and patterned tie. The suit was impeccably cut, and she wondered where he'd gotten it. It looked expensive.

"Hey, there. You look great."

When he glanced up, his mouth hung open like he was about to say something but had been cut off in the middle.

"Is this okay?" She checked out her navy, wraparound dress with the swirly skirt. It hugged her figure and seemed to hide any of the bulges she had.

"It's absolutely amazing. You are gorgeous, Leni."

Heat rushed from her head to her toes at the compliment. "Are we ready to go?"

Dean held out his arm, and she quickly took it, then signed to her mom. "*I'll see you later.*"

"Take your time. The kids and I will be fine. Enjoy yourselves."

They exited the house, and Eleni froze at the sedan sitting in the street. "Whose car?"

"My landlady insisted I couldn't take you out somewhere nice in my old, beat-up truck. She let me use hers. Hope you didn't have your heart set on the torn, Naugahyde seats."

Laughing, Eleni settled in the car. "I can tough it out for the night."

Dean turned the ignition and steered through the streets until they got to The Sands.

"The competition? Is this allowed?" she teased him.

As he helped her get out of the car, he said, "I wanted to take you to a really nice place. However, I didn't want to take you back to work after you'd been there all day, so the Black Pearl was out. I've heard The Captain's Table here is excellent. Have you been here before?"

"A time or two. It's a little pricey for me with the kids. Are you sure you don't want to go down to Rods or the diner on Main Street?"

"In this suit and that dress? No, we are stepping out in style tonight, Ms. Griffin. Whether you like it or not."

"I do like it. Thank you, Mr. Peters."

Dean flinched when she said that, and she wondered why. Did it make him think of his father who'd passed away ten years ago? Maybe she could ask him during dinner.

The hostess escorted them to an outside table overlooking the ocean. The sound of the waves lapping against the shore added to the ambiance. The small table was covered in a white lace tablecloth and had a large votive cup with a flickering candle inside. Space heaters were scattered about, infusing the cool night breeze with warmth.

It wasn't long before a waitress stopped by to get their drink order. Eleni got a sweet tea and Dean nodded for the same.

"Please, don't feel you have to get something non-alcoholic just because I do. I'm okay with other people having a few drinks."

He reached for her hand and stroked his thumb over the skin. "As much as I like a cold beer with my meal every now and then, I don't need it, and I definitely don't want to be driving my landlady's car while under the influence. Honestly, with you, I want all my faculties to be as clear as possible."

Heat rushed to her face, and she lowered her gaze to the menu. Was there something on here that wasn't too expensive? A pasta dish or chicken?

Dean squeezed her hand before releasing it. "Order what you feel like eating or something you haven't tried before but want to. I told you, I have a little saved for a rainy day."

It was like he had read her mind. Or picked up on the fact she was frugal in most everything.

They shared some shrimp and crab dip with fancy crackers for an appetizer, then chatted until her Chicken Marsala and his Porterhouse were served. The food was excellent, though Eleni didn't expect anything else. The Captain's Table and The Black Pearl were the two most expensive restaurants on the island.

An hour later, even though their conversation was non-stop, she still didn't know much more about him than before. His answers to most of her questions about his life before he'd moved here were vague. Was he embarrassed by his past? By the fact he was a maintenance worker? Certainly a respectable job in her mind.

As they splurged on dessert—one she hadn't made, making it even better in her mind—Dean shifted closer and took her hand.

"I have to tell you something."

"You look so serious. Is everything all right?"

His thumb ran over the skin of her hand, sending tingles along her spine. "I've worked for a lot of the other resorts that Yios Corp. owns. I've known the owner, Demitrius Petrakis, forever."

"Family friends, huh?"

Dean nodded. "You could say that. As a favor to him, I came down to work here to check out how the resort is run. He also said I needed to work on my tan."

Eleni laughed but wondered if something had happened to make the owner worry about this particular resort. "So you're a spy of sorts."

CHAPTER FIFTEEN

Dean held his breath as Eleni responded to his revelation.

Her eyes twinkled. "What have you found out?"

At her casual question, his shoulders lowered. "For the most part, it runs well. Aarya does a great job."

"No mention of the assistant manager, huh?"

He stayed silent. The man wasn't terrible at his job, but there was room for lots of improvement in his mind.

"I am going to demand a raise for myself and all the maintenance staff, however."

She squeezed his hand. "You definitely deserve it. I've seen how hard you work."

He grinned. "Thea mentioned you liked watching me. That I had nice muscles."

"Oh, God." Her cheeks turned pink, and she glanced away. "I can't believe she overheard that. Or that she told you."

His thumb stroked her skin, and she squirmed in her seat.

"I'm glad she did." He gazed at her until she blushed even more. Her face was almost crimson now.

"Are you on a spy mission tonight to check out the competition?"

"No, I just wanted somewhere fancy. I may have to tell Vlad about the shrimp and crab dip here, though. It's excellent."

"Actually, he just added some shrimp and crab puffs to the specials menu recently. I've taste tested a few, and they might be better than the dip here. He may have to put them on the menu permanently."

"I haven't tried any of the food in the restaurant since I've been here. Good to know."

Eleni grinned. "Get in good with Vlad, and he'll give you samples every now and then if you stop by the kitchen. He doesn't do it for everyone,"

His first reaction as the owner of the resort was that the chef shouldn't be giving their food away for free. However, now that he'd seen how hard Eleni worked, as well as a number of other employees, he didn't think having them sample a bite here or there was a bad thing. They could give meaningful suggestions on meal choices if asked by guests.

"Have you gone to any of the other resorts and spied on them, too?" She scooped out the last of her chocolate mousse and licked the spoon.

Shivers ran down his spine at the sight of her tongue running along the utensil. What had she asked? Oh, the resorts.

"I'm not an actual spy. This is just a favor for the owner."

"A pretty big favor, considering what you have to do. I hope they're paying you extra for dealing with...some of the staff."

She meant Hugh, although Reva had been a pain in his backside with her personal requests and little tantrums. He didn't care how much she did for Trey while he was in town, Dean and his brother needed to have a talk about his hiring practices.

"I'm getting compensated fine. Thus, my not worrying about the price of this dinner like I know you're doing."

The guilty expression on Eleni's face said it all. "Then, thank you for spending some, hopefully not all, of your compensation on me."

Dean sent her a smile he hoped would assure her that he didn't mind at all. The waitress stopped by and asked if they needed anything else.

"I think we're all set." He glanced at Eleni, who nodded.

Once the check was paid and he'd left a generous tip on the table, he steered Eleni toward the side of the building. "Are you up for a walk along the beach? Unless you need to get back."

"The kids'll be in bed by now and most likely Mom is watching a movie or reading. We should be okay for a little stroll."

Dean took her hand and led her down the walkway that ended at the sand behind the resort.

"Hold on. I need to take these shoes off. They're great for a nice dinner out, not so much for beach walking." She held tightly to his arm as she removed the high heels that made her legs look even more fabulous than ever.

They ambled down to where the surf kissed the sand and headed away from the resort. The silence was comfortable as Eleni nestled against his arm.

"Hey, I forgot to tell you. Hugh gave me a big apology for the nuts. Said it was irresponsible of him to have them around, and he'd make sure to remember about my allergy in the future."

"That's great. I hope he does." Pretty sure it was the word that came from corporate that had him handing out the "I'm sorry".

"Have you had a bad reaction before? What are the symptoms?"

"It depends on where the oil gets or if I eat it. The very first time, I was small, and my mouth swelled up, as well as my throat. My parents got me to the hospital quickly. After that, I was super careful about what I ate."

"So you haven't had a reaction since then?"

Eleni eyed the moon, shining brightly in the night sky. "A few times I got oil on my skin, and it started to swell. But there was one time Sean had eaten peanuts at work and must have gotten the oil on his pants. I probably touched it doing laundry and wiped my fingers across my mouth, because my lips started swelling. Scared me, for sure."

"But he got you to the hospital in time?"

Her eyes lowered to the ground, and she inhaled deeply.

"Eleni?"

When she gazed back up at him, her lips were in a straight line. "Unfortunately, Sean wasn't in any shape to take me anywhere. The kids were babies and already asleep. I didn't want to try and get them in the car and drive myself there, but once you use an Epi Pen you have to seek medical help. So...I took a few Benedryl and hoped for the best."

"Does that work?" His arm circled her shoulder, and he pulled her closer.

"If I had ingested the nuts, no it wouldn't. However, since it had only gotten on my skin, I was able to ride it out. With a really swollen lip and half asleep because of the medicine, but it ended up fine."

Dean wanted to rip into her husband for his stupid negligence, but the man wasn't around. He hated that the kids didn't have a dad, yet who knew what would have happened to Eleni and the children if Sean had continued on the way he was. They could have been killed just as easily in some other incident.

After a while, they circled around and started back the way they'd come. It had been forever since Dean had enjoyed a night like this with a woman. Most wanted whatever he was willing to buy them. Eleni simply wanted to be with him. It was refreshing.

Once on the walkway, she slipped her shoes back on and gazed up at him. "Does the owner expect you to go back to the Cape Cod resort?"

Dean's stomach clenched. "I can if I want to."

She tapped his hand with her finger. "Do you want to?"

If he did, that whole becoming her boyfriend thing would be a moot point. How disappointed would Thea be? Or Xander, since he'd promised to help do dad stuff? They'd started to build a small birdhouse using instructions they'd seen online.

"I thought I would at first. Now, I'm finding Last Chance Beach has some definite advantages over New England."

Eleni's smile grew, and she gave a deep sigh. "The warmer weather, of course."

Was she hoping for him to stick around? What did he want? It was something he needed to think about.

Both his hands found hers as he said, "Definitely warmer. All around."

"You are a saint for helping me with this, Dean." Eleni hugged the man briefly before dragging him along to the back of the house.

"Happy to do it. Not every day you turn nine. Only one year left until double digits."

Eleni swung around and frowned. "Don't remind me. I'm already feeling old, wishing they were babies again."

Dean chuckled as he followed her. Her back yard wasn't big, but there was enough space for some games for the boys Xander had invited. Thea's activities would be inside the house. Thank God, Dean had offered to lead the boys with the events she'd planned.

"Marek said he could stay if you needed help. This is one of the difficult things about having twins that are different genders. If I had two girls, we could all do the same thing. Xander absolutely refused to do hair and nails."

"I don't blame him. Not that I don't like the results of hair and nail work, but I'm not sure I'd enjoy doing them myself. We'll be fine with the sports theme you've got planned out here."

Eleni peeked around, then tugged his head down for a kiss. His arms snaked around her and kept her in place.

"I'll do this every weekend if this is the reward I get." His eyebrows rose and fell comically.

After another quick kiss, she showed him the games she had set up and how to play each of them. "I'll bring the girls out to play, too. Maybe when the boys use the basketball hoop."

"It's too bad you couldn't use some of the resort amenities. They've got the volleyball and tennis courts. That large grassy area near the horseshoe pits. Both pools, not to mention the entire beach front area. I'm sure Vlad would be happy to make up something special for the birthday kids."

Eleni laughed and shook her head. "Are you kidding me? Have you noticed how many children are at the resort? Very few. All of the activities that Reva organizes are geared toward adults. Wealthy adults."

"I know, but it's really slow right now. They should be happy to bring people in, regardless of their usual clientele."

Eleni replaced a few of the bean bags she'd thrown to show Dean how the game worked. "Oh, believe me, I've had tons of ideas for how they could get business in during the slower months. Hugh always makes me feel like I'm stupid for even suggesting it. He said corporate would never approve of anything like that. Since I haven't had many dealings with them, I figured he knew best, so I never mentioned them to Aarya when she took over. The hotel seems to market to rich singles and couples. Not families."

Dean's eyebrows drifted together, and his lips thinned. "That's too bad. They're missing out on some good business and lots of fun."

"I know, but it's not my job to come up with marketing ideas. I just make sure what's already planned runs smoothly. Like today. We need this party to run smoothly."

Rubbing his hands together, Dean inspected the yard. "I've got this part. When are the guests arriving?"

She glanced at her watch. "In about fifteen minutes. Come on into the house and grab something to drink first. I made some food for the kids to nibble on, so they aren't totally jazzed on cake and junk food."

Her mom bustled about the kitchen, getting food on trays and placing them on the kitchen table and the counters. Dean tapped her mom on the shoulder, then gave her a peck on the cheek. Was her mom getting attached to Dean as much as the kids were?

"You'd think you were feeding an army," he said. "How many kids are coming?"

"Four for Xander and four for Thea. We belong to a homeschool group, and these are kids who are in it. There's been some talk in town about building an elementary school, but who knows if it'll ever come about."

Dean snatched a carrot stick. "Most likely, when your kids graduate from high school and you don't need it anymore."

"Exactly. That's just the kind of luck I seem to have."

"Mom, Livy and Kandra are here," Xander shouted, running through the house toward the door.

Eleni took a deep breath. "Showtime."

Thea ran after her brother. Dean stood behind her, his hands on her shoulders. "They're kids. Anything you do will be amazing for them. Just having their friends over will be fun."

His lips touched her neck, and she melted against him. If only they were alone. As it was, her mother was probably watching them from the kitchen.

"Maybe after the kids are all gone, if you still have any energy left, we could walk down to the beach and just sit and watch the ocean."

She spun in his arms. "I'd love that. Depends on how they are once they're hyped up on birthday cake and party goods. I don't want to leave Mom here with two wild monkeys."

Both Marek and Nadine ended up staying to help, and Eleni couldn't help but peek out the window every now and then to see what the boys were up to. She loved how Marek and Dean seemed to get along so well. They kept the boys under control yet energized and having fun at the same time.

She and Nadine were up to their eyeballs in nail polish, plastic jewelry, glitter makeup, and shiny fabric. She'd bought several yards of fancy, but cheap, fabric on her last visit off-island, and the girls were having a ball draping it over themselves in a variety of ways. Pictures were snapped, and Eleni sent them immediately to her printer, so the girls would have a copy to take home with them.

"This was such a great idea," Nadine commented after the girls had all been dolled up. "It's too bad The Pearl doesn't offer something similar. I know so many moms who would love something like this, without having to do all the planning and executing."

"It does look fun." Dean's voice had her spinning. He hovered in the doorway, grinning at the silly antics of the girls. "The boys are ready for cake and ice cream whenever it's good for you. We can run them around the block once or twice if you need more time."

"No, I think we're good. Bring them in."

The next hour was filled with candles, singing, sugar highs, and birthday presents. Dean insisted they both open his gift at the same time.

Eleni gasped when she saw the intricate wooden box with seashells carved on the top.

"I had Ben Hadley make them. I thought you should have a special place to put all your best shells, so they don't get damaged."

Thea rushed over and hugged him tight. Xander, aware his friends were watching him, thrust his hand out and gave a firm shake with his thanks.

"How about Marek and I take them all out to run around the yard if you want a few quiet minutes until their parents get here?" Nadine offered.

Eleni gave her friend a quick hug. "You're amazing. I'll clean up a bit, then come out."

Dean stayed behind to give her a hand. As her mom emptied the trash and took the bag outside, Eleni rushed to Dean and threw her arms around him.

"That is the most thoughtful gift ever, Dean. I love that it isn't some hastily bought present from the store. Thank you."

He touched his lips lightly to hers. "Maybe you can thank me later."

She wrinkled her nose. "The children should be thanking you. It's their gifts."

Another quick kiss. "I like your thank yous better."

A car pulled up, and Eleni reluctantly eased out of his arms. "I've got to say goodbye to the kids."

Once all the kids were gone, as well as Nadine and Marek with theirs, she, Thea, and Xander trooped back into the house. She froze when she got to the kitchen. It looked like there'd never been a party there.

"*How did you clean this up so fast?*" she signed to her mom.

"I had help." Mom said and pointed to Dean coming in from the back door.

"Dean, you didn't need to do all this."

He shrugged. "It's what I do all day long. I've got it down pat at this point."

"I know, and you shouldn't have to do it on your day off."

He narrowed his gaze at the kids. "I was hoping if I helped enough, I might get offered another piece of your birthday cake later."

That meant he was planning to stick around for a while. Not something she'd object to.

He ended up staying through dinner, delivery pizza—she couldn't even fathom cooking anything—and a movie. She'd insisted the kids get pajamas on first and brush their teeth. They piled on the floor while she and Dean occupied the couch. Mom had begged off and retired to her room for the night to read.

The movie was goofy, but whenever she peeked at Dean, his smile was real. Maybe he enjoyed seeing the kids as they watched, or perhaps it was his hand that kept sneaking over to rub her thigh.

Eleni went boneless and rested against Dean's shoulder, not caring what the actors on the screen were doing. Being next to him, soaking up his warmth and strength, gave her the best feeling. One she hadn't experienced in a long time. Maybe ever.

Ever? She'd loved Sean. She had. Over the years, some of those feelings may have dwindled as he sunk deeper and deeper into the bottle. Sometimes, it was difficult to dredge up the feelings she'd had for him once upon a time.

Then, she'd look at Thea and Xander and know they'd been there. But it was time to move on. Five years was a long time to be alone. Was Dean someone she could count on to stick with her? And the kids?

His presence next to her now, as well as the entire day, seemed to indicate he would. He hadn't once complained about the kids, the noise, or the long day. Nothing non-verbal either. She knew how to read people. Often, someone might say they were fine doing something, but their posture, body language, and facial expressions told the real truth.

"I think they're both out cold, Leni." Dean's voice tickled her ear, and she roused from her sleepy state.

"Mmm." Snuggling closer, she closed her eyes again. She could get used to having him right here.

"Stay right here. I'll put them in bed." He rose from the couch, and she started to object, but he tucked a pillow under her head and kissed her cheek. One at a time, he picked up the children and hustled them into their room.

She should be helping him, tucking them in and kissing them goodnight. She'd do it before she went to bed. Thoughts of having Dean next to her as she slept crept through her, causing all sorts of delicious feelings throughout her body.

When he finally came back, he scooped her up, and she gave a tiny shriek. "What are you doing?"

"You can't stay awake either. You've had a busy day and have to work in the morning. Time for you to sleep, too."

Luckily, she'd thrown on loose yoga pants and a sweatshirt when the kids had gotten in pajamas. She'd been self-conscious at first, but if Dean was planning to stick around, he had to know she wasn't always pulled together.

He set her on her feet inside her bedroom and gave her a chaste kiss. Twining her arms around his neck, she deepened the kiss. God, she wanted him to stay. But with the kids here, not to mention her mother...not a good idea.

"I wish—"

He pressed his finger against her lips. "Lots of wishes. Tonight, you need rest. We can talk about wishes later. I'll let myself out and lock up behind me."

"You're so fabulous. Thank you."

The expression that crossed his face was strange and unreadable.

As he turned to go, she caught his hand. "Next Thursday is Thanksgiving. Do you have plans? With your brother? Anyone else?"

"My brother's in Europe currently."

"I'd love it if you had Thanksgiving with us. Thea and Xander would be thrilled if you joined us. My mother's already talking about making you some baklava. It was her grandmother's recipe."

His smile lit up the dark room. "How can I turn down homemade baklava?"

Eleni crossed her arms over her chest. "I was hoping there might be another reason you'd want to stop in."

He stroked his fingers down her cheeks and touched his forehead to hers. "The number one reason I visit is right here." His kiss was light but powerful. He claimed her lips, and she happily surrendered.

Too soon, he backed away and paused at her bedroom door. "I'd be happy to join you for Thanksgiving. Seems, because of you, I have so much more to be thankful for."

CHAPTER SIXTEEN

Dean tapped away at his computer, his eyes darting to the clock every few minutes. He was due at Eleni's for Thanksgiving dinner soon, but he'd wanted to get some ideas jotted down before he forgot.

Hugh might not have wanted anything to do with Eleni's ideas about family packages for the resort, but Dean had a feeling they'd be changing all that soon enough. He couldn't completely blame Hugh for the lack of children's programming. Reva was in charge of activities, and marketing had never set up a family package. More so, he and Trey had never expressed much interest in the younger set.

Now, he couldn't understand why he'd never seen how much fun children could be. Well, sure he could. It was because he wasn't able to have any. In his limited mind, he'd never thought beyond having biological children of his own, yet there were so many children everywhere who needed parents and didn't have them. Could he offer something at the resort for that demographic, also?

He finished typing the plans for a children's club that could take place during school vacations. Maybe he could get teachers involved to run it. But would they want to give up their vacation time to be with kids? Perhaps, if there was some incentive. Like a free vacation week at any of their resorts worldwide at a later date?

He'd have to give this some thought. It wasn't anything he wanted leaked to the competition, and they hadn't found the culprit yet. Hugh had stuck him on a few more overnight shifts, but Dean simply took it in stride and used each opportunity to do some snooping. Unfortunately, aside from some suspicious expenditures, he hadn't stumbled across any solid information.

Scooping up the flowers he'd bought for the table, along with an extra bag of rolls, he trotted down his stairs and strolled along the street and around the corner to Eleni's house. He smirked when he thought of another project he'd had on his mind lately.

"Mr. Dean's here!" Xander yelled loud enough for them to hear on the mainland. Eleni cringed and rushed over to take the flowers from him.

"Sorry. He hasn't seen you in a few days, and he's excited. You've been busy lately."

After retrieving a vase from an upper cabinet, she filled it with water and arranged the flowers inside. As she placed the vase in the middle of the dining table, he sidled up behind her.

"I've been working extra hours, so I'd have today off. Thursday is typically my day to work."

"Oh, I'm sorry. I didn't even think. It's one of the conditions I needed met when I took the job. Thanksgiving, Christmas, and Easter off, so I can be with my kids."

He leaned in for a quick kiss, then stepped back. "Smart woman. I should have you negotiate my next job."

Her head tilted, her eyebrows bunching together. "Are you looking for another job?"

"Not at the moment. There are lots of perks where I currently work."

Eleni glanced around. Her mother and the kids were in the other room. "What kind of perks? Are they anything I should be negotiating for?"

"I get to work with this incredibly sexy woman who drives me out of my mind. I don't think she even knows what she does to me."

Her eyes gleamed. "Really? Perhaps you should tell her."

The sound of the children running through the house jolted him back to reality. "I'm hoping to real soon."

"I have a feeling she'll appreciate it."

Thea shuffled in with Cuddles in her arms. "Hi, Mr. Dean. Do you like turkey? Because that's what we're having today."

"What? Here I'd gotten my hopes up for hamburgers and hot dogs."

"We could have those tomorrow. You can come over tomorrow, right?" Thea peeked at her mom and nodded.

Eleni grinned. "Mr. Dean is always welcome here, Thea. However, there might be times he'd like a little peace and quiet. This is a very busy household."

The little girl's eyes widened, and the corners of her mouth turned down. "We can be quiet here, too."

Taking pity on the child, he tugged on her ponytail. "I'm happy to come around anytime someone wants me here."

Xander zoomed through the room and skidded to a halt in front of him. "I always want you here. We men need to stick together."

"I want him here, too," Thea whined like she'd been outdone.

"I think it's unanimous. We all want you here," Eleni joined in. "Now, it's time to set the table. The turkey is just about ready to come out of the oven."

"Let me help you with that." He meandered through the kitchen and gave Georgie a kiss on the cheek as she mashed potatoes.

"Eleni said you liked baklava. I hope so because I made a ton."

He faced her and signed, "*Thank you. You're the best.*"

Eleni and Georgie bustled about putting bowls and platters on the table the twins were now setting. Dean grabbed the oven mitts, carefully removed the turkey from the oven, and placed it on the stove.

"Eleni, did you want me to carve this?" He closed the oven door and turned it off.

"Yes, please, if you don't mind. The carving knife is in the drawer." She tucked her hair behind her ear and looked around the kitchen. "What am I forgetting?"

The kids and Georgie were in the dining room, so he tugged her close. "To kiss me. Never forget that."

They shared a quick kiss before the kids' voices broke them apart. "Maybe we can finish that later?"

He nodded. "Count on it."

Once the food was all on the table and everyone had taken their seats, Georgie held out her hands for Eleni and Xander to take. He and Thea joined in as Georgie blessed the food.

"Thank you, Lord, for all you've provided for us this day. For the scrumptious feast we have before us. For giving Eleni a job that feeds and clothes us. For this comfortable home we live in. For all our good friends, especially Dean, who is sharing this with us today. And for all the blessings you've bestowed on us. Amen."

"Amen."

As food was passed around, Dean reflected on Georgie's prayer. Here was a family that barely made ends meet, that lived in a tiny cottage with worn furniture, who shopped at bargain stores and thrift shops, and who stretched every dollar they had. Yet they acted like they were the richest people in the world.

He slipped his hand under the table and tapped Eleni's leg. When she glanced over, he whispered, "Thank you so much for making me feel like part of your family today. You have no idea how special this is for me."

Her genuine smile warmed him deep inside. "I'm glad you're here. We all are. You've become special to us, as well."

Xander chattering away about the skateboard he wanted for Christmas broke the spell, but Dean couldn't be happier to listen to what the kids were hoping Santa would bring. He wondered if he'd have caught the culprit by then. Hopefully...and yet, he almost didn't want to because then he would have an excuse to stay here.

The meal was excellent, and Dean stuffed himself on Georgie's baklava after. A walk was in order to try and work off all the calories they'd eaten.

The late afternoon was breezy, so they added sweaters and strolled the neighborhood. A few of the houses already had Christmas decorations up, and the kids made it a point to comment on them.

"When can we put our Christmas decorations up, Mom?" Thea asked hopefully.

Eleni laughed. "I'd like to wait at least a week. Maybe next Sunday, if I can find time to get into the attic." The little girl nodded and skipped away to catch up to her grandmother.

Dean snagged her hand and stroked her skin. "I can help if you need it. How much stuff do you have? Do you light up the entire house?"

Her mouth tightened, and she shook her head. "No, I wish we could. The kids bug me every year to put a huge display up. The problem is, even if I had the money to buy all those lights, the electric bill would kill me. I hate letting them down, but I don't want the kids to worry about money at their age."

"They've both got quite a list for Santa. Do they still believe? I can't remember how old I was when I learned the truth."

"The truth of what? Is there something about Santa I should know?" Her eyes gleamed with mischief. He loved this silly side of her. It brought out the kid in him again.

He slung his arm around her shoulder and pressed a quick kiss to her cheek. She gazed at him like he was a superstar. How had he ever deserved that?

"I'm not sure if they still believe, but they could be playing along, thinking they'll get more if they do. Obviously, I can't get them everything on their list, but I'll try and get a few things."

Dean wanted to run out and buy them all whatever they needed and wanted. It wasn't like he had any use for most of what he earned. Especially not living on this island. But even if Eleni knew of his wealth, he doubted she'd want him spoiling the kids with material possessions. She valued family, hard work, love, and friends. All things he would have scoffed at three months ago as being soft and emotional. Now, he knew better. Eleni and her family had shown him that.

"Eleni, Dean," Georgie called out. "The kids wanted to watch that movie tonight. It's on in a bit. I'll take them home. You and Dean should spend some time together without the wee ones. I'll get them in bed once the movie is over. Don't rush back."

Thea and Xander skipped over and hugged him and their mother, then raced back to the house. Georgie trekked at a slower pace behind them.

"I think my mother wants us to spend some time together. Alone. What do you think?"

Dean grinned at her. "I think Santa needs to bring your mother a very large Christmas present."

They strolled through the small downtown area, where some of the businesses had strung up lights and begun putting wreaths on the decorative lamp posts.

"This island has a special feel to it. Quaint and homey, yet it's far from boring."

Eleni sighed. "It's grown a lot in the last ten years. As much as I need the tourists showing up so I have a job and can afford to live here, I sometimes wish it wouldn't change that much."

"I understand what you're saying." Tourism was vital for the resort to thrive, but would too much of it kill the reason people came here to begin with?

As they passed his apartment, Eleni clung to his side. "I really don't want to go back yet. I'm enjoying my time alone with you too much. Does that make me an awful mother?"

He pressed a kiss to her hair. "No, it makes you human and a woman who has needs beyond that of her children." His needs started howling inside to be let out. "Would you like to come up and see my place? I can make us hot chocolate or tea if you'd like some."

"That sounds wonderful."

As they climbed the stairs, he asked, "What sounds wonderful? The hot chocolate or the tea?"

"Coming up to see your place."

Those words gave him hope. He unlocked the door and let her go in first. "It's not the Ritz, but it has a bed and a bathroom. I don't need much more. I have this fabulous lady who's been feeding me almost every night."

Eleni examined the large living and kitchen area, then ambled to the couch. "It's nice to be somewhere that I don't have to worry about cleaning up or be reminded there's another two loads of laundry to do."

As he shrugged out of his coat, she took hers off and set it over the arm of the couch. He settled beside her and tugged until she rested against his chest.

"No cooking, cleaning, or laundry allowed here from you. Your job is to relax."

She gazed up at him with desire in her eyes. This might be trouble. He'd been holding himself in check with her since the first time they kissed.

"There isn't anything else I need to do while I'm here?" She cocked her head.

"What would you like to do?"

She kneeled up next to him and cupped his face. "This." Her mouth touched and teased his, and he lost all control. Crushing her to him, he returned her kisses, stroking his hands down her arms, her back, over her hair. He couldn't get enough.

Like teenagers sitting in the back of a darkened movie theater, they explored and enjoyed. Eleni's responses were so passionate and filled with emotion, he caught on fire.

"I know your injury kept you from having kids—" her breathless voice turned him on so much, "—but does it keep you from enjoying a woman in every way?"

Was she asking what he thought she was? Her eyes were giving him the green light.

"Oh, I can enjoy that perfectly fine. Would you like a demonstration?"

At her nod, he scooped her in his arms and carried her toward the bedroom.

"I'd love a demonstration, but you might need to repeat it a few times since I'm a very slow learner."

CHAPTER SEVENTEEN

*E*leni snuggled up against Dean as they wandered along the beach.

"Your mother deserves a special award for taking the kids shopping today."

"She didn't want to wait too late in December or it gets ridiculously crowded. As it is, I'm sure Summerville is busy today. But the kids have saved some money and wanted to do their own Christmas shopping this year. They can't really buy me something if I'm with them."

Dean's arms tightened, and he stopped to kiss her. His lips on hers made her want more of him. Since a week ago at Thanksgiving, when they'd gone to his apartment, she'd tried to squeeze in more time with him. Alone time.

This morning, for instance, when she'd shown up at his place with a thermos of coffee and homemade cinnamon rolls. He'd greeted her at the door in only a pair of pajama pants. Her heart had needed a few minutes to recover.

Then, Dean had set the food on the counter and whisked her into his bedroom, the sheets still warm from him sleeping in them. They'd heated them up even more. The coffee had been cold by the time they got around to drinking it. Neither one of them had minded.

After lunch on Main Street, they'd biked up to the lighthouse and strolled along the sand. Very different when Thea and Xander weren't yelling to take a look at what they'd found every two minutes.

Her gaze swung to The Hideaway as they wandered close, and she sighed.

"What's wrong?" Dean stroked her cheek with his thumb. Oh, Lord, she loved when he touched her like that.

She shook her head and shrugged. "Oh, nothing. I heard the house sold." There was already staging leaning against the porch and lumber stacked in the yard.

His eyebrows dipped down. "Hmm. At least now it'll have someone living in it."

"Maybe not. Lots of these cottages get sold to people who rent them out by the week, especially the waterfront ones. Occasionally, you might get someone who wants it for the whole summer season, but rarely does the owner live there. That house needs a family who will love it."

Standing behind her, he wrapped his arms around her waist. "What would you do to it if you owned it?

"If I could do anything I wanted? Like a fantasy or winning the lottery?"

"Or if I bought it for you." His breath near her ear had her shivering and not from the cool breeze.

Laughing, she twisted her head to see his face. He was grinning. "Did you buy it for me?"

"Maybe."

She tipped her chin up, so she could kiss him. "Thank you, kind sir."

Facing back to focus her attention to the house, she envisioned it from when she'd seen it years ago. "If I'm dreaming and get carte blanche, then I'd definitely redo the kitchen. All updated appliances and a new floor. I'd have someone redo the cabinets in a light stain. The cabinets are gorgeous and had this beautiful stained glass in some of them. That's where you put your nice dishes."

"Do you have nice dishes?"

"Smart Alec. I do, but they aren't what I use every day with the kids. You saw them on Thanksgiving."

"So you'd spruce up the kitchen. What else?"

"I love the wraparound porch, but it needs fixing. The one above it in the main bedroom is sagging, as well. Then, new siding."

"Vinyl siding?"

She flinched. "Oh, no. You have to have the wooden shingles to make it look like a cottage and to match the rest of the homes on the island."

"What are the floors like in there?"

"Well, there're a few carpets that would have to go. With the sand from the beach, the kids would drag in, I'd be vacuuming all day. The hardwood would need to be resanded, then I'd add hardwood or some nice laminate in the bedrooms. And the kitchen..."

"What about the kitchen?"

"I'd love to have some large ceramic tiles in there. And the bathrooms, too. In the summer when it gets super hot and humid here, standing on the tile floors barefoot would be heavenly."

"So, that's it? New floors and an updated kitchen."

"Not so fast, buster. If I'm dreaming, I'm dreaming big. Every room would need to be sanded and painted."

"What colors would you like?"

It was fun standing here with Dean's arms around her, creating fantasies. "Not white. I always find white walls too sterile and cold. Something soft and warm. It needs to feel homey. Welcoming."

Dean kissed her cheek. "I think any home you're in would be warm and welcoming."

"Soft buttery yellow."

"Yellow?"

"For the kitchen, with navy blue accents. Then lavender for Thea's room and a pale blue for Xander's. It would be so great if they had their own room. I'm not sure how much longer I can keep them together."

Dean's hand reached out and pointed to The Hideaway. "But you've got this great place. Does Georgie have a favorite color?"

She nodded. "Yes, peach. Mom loves how calming and peaceful a soft peach is."

"And what about you? What's your room going to look like?"

"Hmm." She tipped her head and pictured what she'd like in there. "Maybe sage or a really light periwinkle."

Dean's arms stiffened. "What's sage or periwinkle?"

Eleni chuckled. "Sage is a soft, light green. Almost a mossy color. Periwinkle is a light bluish purple."

As she inhaled Dean's manly scent, she wondered if he'd ever share a room with her. Not just for a few hours but permanently. In her dreams, he absolutely would.

"This all sounds perfect, Leni. What else would you have in your fantasy house? What kind of furniture."

"You know I have a soft spot for antiques. I'd probably go and buy up half of Haddie's stock at Secondhand Antiques. Maybe I'd have Ben make some custom furniture, too. Dressers and large armoires, if Haddie didn't have something I liked."

"Are there no closets in the bedrooms?"

"I think I remember them being kind of small, so I'd need extra space. Unless my fantasy consisted of a closet that grew as you used it."

Dean laughed. "I guess you'd have to contact Dr. Who to get that kind of work done."

"Closet space is great, but one of the things I remember loving about the main bedroom was the window seat. I'd fix that all up nice, with cushions that matched the bedspread and curtains. I could sit in it and read while watching the ocean and listening to the waves."

As his arms tightened around her, he spun until they faced the ocean. "Is that window seat big enough for two?"

She grinned at him. "It could be if we were creative."

Dean ran his hands over her back until she pressed fully against him. "I can be creative."

Now, he was speaking her language. The kids were away most of the day with her mother. What else did they have to do?

She touched her lips to his. "Maybe you could show me."

Dean rested his arm on the back of Eleni's chair as Marek stood and offered his hand to Nadine.

"Would you care to dance, beautiful lady?"

Nadine made a surprised face. "Who? Me? Why, I'd love to, kind sir."

Dean laughed at the antics of the happily married couple now swaying to the music on the dance floor. Sundown was a casual restaurant on the ocean, near the pier. It had soft music, and often local musicians played guitar or keyboard. He preferred that to a few of the other bars, where it was so loud you couldn't even hear the person next to you.

They'd come here a few times when they'd gotten someone to watch all the kids. Tonight, Vlad was keeping Georgie company with a sleepover for Kandra and Livy.

"I hope the kids are good tonight and aren't too much for Mom," Eleni said as her hand tapped to the beat of the music. Dean wasn't much of a dancer, yet he still itched to hold her in his arms.

"I think your mother is happy that you're getting out. Vlad is frosting on the cake."

The smile on Eleni's face was the most beautiful thing he'd ever seen. He loved when she was happy. Making her that was his new number one goal.

"It is nice to get away from the house every now and again, especially with good friends."

"Good friends." He squeezed her hand, remembering exactly how good they'd been together. Unfortunately, they'd need to go their separate ways once they got back tonight. Eleni was responsible for all four kids. It was Marek and Nadine's turn for a quiet night alone. They were warming up on the dance floor right now.

"Thank you again for helping us put the Christmas tree up. It was so much faster with an extra set of hands."

Dean caressed her cheek. "It's been a long time since I've decorated a tree. I appreciate being included. You always make me feel like one of the family."

Wasn't that the truth. Between her mother and her children, being at Eleni's brought a feeling of home that he hadn't felt in too many years. Often, Maggie arranged for someone to put up and decorate a tree for him just so he'd have one there. But he'd never been involved. Not since he was much younger, and his dad had still been alive.

Dean picked up his soda and took a sip. Nadine had a fancy drink and Marek had a beer, but he didn't feel right drinking in front of Eleni, not with all she'd confided in him about her husband.

"Do you want to order another appetizer?" Eleni asked as she nibbled on the last nacho in the tray. "You were eyeing those pretzels with the cheese dip."

"You're too observant. I can't get away with anything around you." She knew his entire work schedule, when and where he ate, how often he took a short break, and even when his hip was bothering him. Which made the fact she still didn't know exactly who he was more pronounced. He needed to tell her and soon.

Once he and Trey set a few traps, he'd let Eleni know what was going on. Not that he was in any hurry to find the culprit. The most recent marketing hadn't gone anywhere, so maybe the person stealing it had decided enough was enough and given up.

Marek and Nadine sat down and cooled off with their drinks.

"Your friend, Hugh, is chatting up Cindy Turner over there," Nadine said, her chin tilting in the direction of the corner.

Dean glanced over to where the assistant manager cozied up with a voluptuous woman in a corner booth. "Do I know her?"

Eleni shook her head. "She's a long-time islander. Works in the snack shop at The Sands. I thought she had better taste than that."

Another person to look into. He couldn't access much information on someone who didn't work for Yios, but it was a start. Possibly a link.

"Dean wants some pretzels and cheese," Eleni said. "Should we get something else, too?"

Nadine grinned. "How about some of the loaded potato skins? I love how much bacon they put on them."

Dean waved his hand at the waitress and put in the order. The singer had started a sultry ballad, and Eleni swayed to the beat. He needed to man up and dance.

"Would you care to join me on the dance floor?"

Eleni's mouth curled up in surprise. "I'd love to. Are you sure?"

"I wouldn't have asked if I wasn't."

As they made their way over to the empty space, Dean circled his arm around her shoulder. "It's a great excuse to get you in my arms in public."

"I'm sorry about tonight. Nadine mentioned they'd take the kids to their house soon to reciprocate."

Their feet stepped side to side as his hand brushed along her lower back and hers combed through the hair at his nape.

"The kids seemed excited about seeing the Christmas lights along the island. Not to mention the boat parade."

"We'll wait for the lights for another few weeks. If you drive around the island right before Christmas, so many more houses have decorated. Will you come with us?"

Dean shrugged, "I don't see why not." Unless they found who'd been responsible for stealing their marketing ideas. Even then, did he have to return to the rat race? He'd been running Yios Corp. from Last Chance Beach for four months now. The company had been thriving, and Dean had somehow managed to work a full-time maintenance job at the same time. How much more could he get done if he wasn't cleaning toilets?

It was something he really needed to think about. Make plans for.

Eleni twisted her head and chuckled. "Must be Ocean Pearl day at Sundown tonight. Reva's here, too."

Swirling Eleni in a circle, he peeked around until he saw the Activities Director sitting at the bar. Hair and makeup was even more outrageous than when she was working. She was in full flirt mode as she chatted up the bartender.

Wouldn't Trey be heartbroken?

Truthfully, his brother wouldn't care. The poor woman was just one in a line of many that Trey used. It was hard to feel sorry for her, though, with the way she treated him.

Even though Reva was working it tonight, he had a feeling, with all the pictures he'd seen in her office, if Trey showed up in town, the bartender would be yesterday's news.

CHAPTER EIGHTEEN

*H*is phone rang just as Dean stepped inside his apartment. He glanced at it first, and when he saw it was Trey, swiped to answer.

"Hey, little brother. How's Europe?"

"It's great, but I'm back in the Boston office."

"Everything okay?" Dean had kept track of the business, and nothing had seemed amiss in the last few days. Maggie would have informed him of any problems immediately.

"It's all fine, except I do actually work as CFO of this place. Sometimes, I have to use my office."

Dean chuckled. "I've been able to do my job without mine. It's very freeing, as you would know as the king of delegating work. I learned at your side, which is why I've been able to stay down here as long as I have."

"Which brings me to my next topic."

"Next? Did we have a first topic, other than hello and how are you?"

"Not really. But seriously, Dean, what gives with the island life? You've been a hermit for the last twenty years."

"I haven't been a hermit. I've occasionally come out of my cave. If I must be labeled, I'd prefer troglodyte." Dean could feel Trey rolling his eyes.

"Whatever we call you, you've suddenly emerged and become human."

"Who told you that? They'd be lying. Ask anyone I work with. They'll tell you I barely speak to any other staff and definitely not to guests." It wasn't false. Eleni and her family and Marek and Nadine were the only ones he's spent any time chatting with. Plus, he had to give his brother a hard time or he'd suspect something was up.

"That's too bad. I would have liked to see you actually interacting with other people. Or those kids you went trick or treating with. But back to the point of your being on Last Chance Beach. Have you gotten any closer to our little marketing thief?"

"Not really. I think we need to lay some bait. Maybe pass around some info to different people and see what turns up. Fake info, of course. Not the changes I really want to make."

"You mentioned changes before. What exactly are you considering?"

"It's too much to discuss right now, and I still need to do some research to see how it'll all work." He wasn't ready to share his kids club idea with Trey quite yet. His brother would have him committed. But once he knew for certain that Eleni felt the same way as he did? Yeah, he'd be yelling from the rooftops.

"Okay, so who do we send information to? I've got the list of staff right here."

Dean booted up his laptop and opened to his staff file. "Even though I think Aarya is excellent at her job, I can't discount her. She lives pretty comfortably on the island. It could be her husband's job, but without getting into their bank accounts, I have no way of knowing."

"So Aarya gets some misleading info. And Hugh? He's next in charge?"

SECRETS UNDER THE SUN

"Yup, he's high on my list. There are also a few women he's constantly flirting with that could be getting some bedtimes stories from him without the man even realizing what he's doing."

"Great. When does he have time to do his job?"

"That's a topic for another conversation. The next suspect is Reva or Chuck. She schedules activities for the guests, while he coordinates resort events. They both have access to the marketing info, as well as the front desk managers."

"Seriously? Reva? I think she'd be grateful that I got her such a cushy position. I'd hate not to have her company when I visit the island."

"I thought you had a whole list of island girls."

Trey snorted. "I do, but Reva tops the list."

"There might be one of the staff in the financial office who works on the budget when we have new marketing."

"So, it's not a short list, but still manageable. What about the administrative assistant to Aarya and Hugh? She'd have perfect placement to see the plans."

"Eleni Griffin? No, it's not her."

"Why do you say that? She has access."

"I know it's not her. There's no way she'd ever do something like this. Besides, if she was getting paid to sabotage us, she's not using the money anywhere."

"And how do you know this, Dean? Have you looked at *her* bank account?"

"No, of course not. But the woman lives paycheck to paycheck. She's got secondhand furniture in her house. Her car is ten years old, and she's as frugal as they come. She's got no extra income streaming her way. Believe me."

"I do believe you. I'm simply wondering how you know so much about this woman."

Dean took a deep breath. He wasn't ready to spill his guts to his brother yet. "I've been here for almost four months. I've gotten to know the staff pretty well."

"You just said you never talked to them."

Darn, he had said that. "There are a few I've gotten friendly with."

"To the point of knowing what kind of furniture they have inside their house?"

Dean cleared his throat. "Can we get back to business?"

Trey chuckled, and Dean wanted to throttle him right through the phone. "So how old is this Eleni Griffin?"

"Um…mid to late thirties." He knew exactly how old she was but wouldn't share that with Trey.

"Married?"

"Her husband died five years ago."

"Ah, so you think she's innocent because of a sob story."

"It's not Leni. Take my word for it."

Another chuckle. "Leni, is it? Exactly how well have you gotten to know her, dear brother? Methinks you didn't need my list of ladies, because you already found one of your own."

"Leni lives with her deaf mother and two children. She isn't the type who'd ever sell secrets. She's loyal to the core."

"Oh, boy. A mom and two kids. You are sending me spiraling today, Deano. I thought maybe you had a hot little number keeping you warm at night, but to hear you say there's a mom and kids in the deal. I am intrigued. We have got to get this mystery solved, so I can visit and check them all out."

Dean expelled a breath and clenched his jaw. "Fine, let's figure this out, so we can get it over with."

Then, he'd have to tell Eleni the truth and hope for the best.

As she passed by the private road that led to The Hideaway, Eleni peeked through the trees. Several trucks sat in the driveway, including a blue vintage one that looked like Ben Hadley's. Had he been hired to do work on the house?

A few minutes later, she pulled into the shell-filled driveway of Secondhand Antiques and climbed out of her car. The four children tumbled from their seats and scattered to find the items on their list near the large red barn. Eleni scooped up the box with the ornaments and wreaths she'd made and sauntered inside.

Kat stood next to the register, her laptop open.

"Working the real job?"

Kat laughed. "Someone's got to pay the bills around here. Are those the wreaths and kissing balls for this weekend?"

Eleni held up a wreath made from white pine branches that Dean and the kids had helped her collect from different locations on the island. With a few pinecones, decorative, colored balls, and a bow, it looked nice.

"I made a dozen using these branches and a dozen with spruce for a slightly different look and scent. Same with the kissing balls."

"I love all the accents you put on them."

Eleni shrugged. "It's amazing what you can get at the dollar store. I have more in the car. I imagine you'll be inundated with people checking out all the Christmas lights, so I doubt this is enough. I can make more, but Haddie said she had other donations coming, too."

"You do so much for us already, Eleni. I'm not sure how you manage with your job and the kids. Plus, today, you have all four of them."

"I gave them a scavenger hunt to do while they're here. I hope you don't mind."

"I think it's great how you mix basic curriculum with the island's history. Not sure I could do that. If Ben and I have kids, I hope that new school is built by then."

"Um...Ben. Is he working on The Hideaway? I thought I saw his truck in the driveway on my way over."

"Yep, he's been over there every day for the past few weeks."

Eleni felt the sinking in her stomach, which was ridiculous. She never could have afforded that place, no matter how many extra hours she put in. The taxes alone were most likely more than her salary.

"Do you know who bought the place?"

Kat shrugged. "You can ask him yourself. He just pulled in."

"I'll go get the rest of the wreaths." Eleni darted back to her car and pulled out the boxes she'd stuffed the kissing balls in.

Ben shuffled over. "Need some help getting this inside the barn?"

"That would be great, Ben. Thanks."

He hefted two of the larger boxes and strode toward the red building.

Eleni picked up the last box, then tucked the box of desserts under her arm. Inside the barn, she placed the wreaths on a table and the desserts on the back sideboard. When she spun back around, Ben was stealing a kiss from Kat. They were an awfully cute couple. It reminded her of the kisses Dean always tried to get from her whenever the kids turned their heads.

"Hey, Eleni, did you make any extra desserts for the grunt labor? I'm always happy to sample to make sure nothing's poisoned." His gaze roamed to the sideboard.

"That's completely up to Haddie and Kat if they want to share. Um...did I see your truck at The Hideaway on my way over here?" Stupid question. Kat had just said he'd been working there.

"Yeah. Man, that's some work being done. And fast."

"Who bought the place?"

Ben shrugged and reached down to scratch Boomer on the neck. "I'm not sure. Some rich city guy. I've only dealt with his assistant. Or I suppose it could be her assistant. The lady refers to the owner as 'my employer' or 'the owner', so it's anyone's guess."

Great. Big city person. Doubtful the cottage would be filled with love and family. Most likely, it would be spoiled beach bums looking for a quick hook up. Or squealing women getting drunk while lamenting their boring lives and unfaithful husbands.

"Well, looks like no expense has been spared. They've got locals hired to redo floors, walls, and even a new roof. I've been contracted to fix the porch and upstairs deck and refinish all the woodwork. That place sure does have beautiful bones."

"I know. I've seen it. I'm glad they aren't just gutting it and starting fresh. I hope they keep the charm of the old house."

Ben nodded. "Oh, definitely old island charm. I've got special orders for a large bed frame, some bureaus, and a few armoires. Lots of shelving going in the main bedroom closet, too.

"So they'll probably rent it out to large groups."

"That'd be my guess. The dining room table they want me to make will seat eight and ten with an extension."

"It sounds beautiful. I hope I'll be able to see it someday."

Ben tipped his head toward the box she'd brought. "Save me a few of those, and I'll give you a private tour once it's done."

Eleni laughed, though she wished the house wasn't going to someone else. "I'll make you a batch just for yourself."

Kat cleared her throat. "Which he'll share with me, correct?"

Ben looked sheepish. "I guess."

"Do you know when the cottage will be finished?"

"It's a rush job. They got people pulling double and weekend shifts to get it done. I think the owner is hoping for Christmas or New Year's."

"Let me know when it's done. I'd love to take you up on that offer of a tour. That house has always spoken to me."

Kat fiddled with the register and handed Eleni an envelope. "Here's for the wreaths and decorations. Really appreciate your making so many. Gram loves what you do and that she's helping a family in need. The cookies are an added bonus for the workers. I hate to see Gram slaving over the stove at her age, but she'd insist on doing it, too. This way she doesn't have to."

Eleni said her goodbyes and went outside to round up the kids. Family in need. Yeah, that pretty much described them. Truthfully, they didn't need for much. They had the important things in life. And now that Dean had gotten involved with them, Eleni was getting even more of her needs met.

Maybe if she didn't assign projects this week, the kids could get to bed early tonight. That would leave her free to take a little walk back to Dean's. He gave her everything and then some.

She didn't need a house on the beach when she had a man who showed her what love and caring was about. Neither of them had said the words, but Eleni felt those emotions deep in her heart. She hoped Dean did, too.

CHAPTER NINETEEN

*A*s much as Dean loved being here on the island and spending time with Eleni and her family every night, he'd confess he wasn't a fan of cleaning up vomit. It was still two weeks before Christmas, but already the revelers were a little too much into the Christmas spirits.

Trey had sent an e-mail to all of the intended targets with a different promo plan in each. He'd made sure to mention the information was to be kept absolutely to themselves until they finalized everything. Now, they needed to wait. Nothing had shown up yet at the competition, but it hadn't been that long.

In the meantime, he'd snooped in some of the offices during his overnight shifts. The one Hugh still insisted giving him at least once a week.

It was almost quitting time for him, so he rinsed out the mop and bucket and rolled it down the hall to put it away. Reva clicked along behind him, then paused as he tucked his tools in the closet.

"Maintenance man, whose name I always forget?"

"Dean. It's Dean." He pointed to his name tag that had rested on his chest for four months.

"Right. Dean." She waved her freshly manicured nails in the air. "So, it's close to Christmas. I'll bet someone like you could use a little extra cash. Am I right?"

"Did you want to hire me to do something? I work for the resort. I get paid to do anything you need me to here." He sure as heck wasn't going to her house to hang Christmas lights.

"Yes, I understand. I just need a little errand run." She lifted a manilla envelope and held it out. "I need you to take this over to the bar by the marina and deliver it to a friend."

"Why can't you do it?"

Her head swiveled, her hair puffing out to the sides as she checked the hallway. "I have so many things to do here with all the Christmas Festival people arriving. I figured you'd have some time. Aren't you off right about now?"

She couldn't remember his name, but she knew what his scheduled hours were? This lady was a dingbat. Something was up with her.

"You're going to pay me to deliver this? How much?" Let's see what she thought his time was worth.

"I'll give you fifty dollars if you can get there by six. My friend is a bartender at Sundown, and that's when he gets off."

He glanced at his watch. Five twenty-five. Not that he needed the money, but Reva was acting strange. Stranger than usual, anyway.

"Sure, I guess I can do it."

After peeking around the hallway again, she tucked a fifty-dollar bill into the flap of the envelope and handed it to him.

"My friend's name is Bob. Tall, dark, good looking. You can't miss him."

All the bartenders at that bar also wore name tags. He'd been there several times with Eleni, Marek, and Nadine.

"Okay, go, go." She waved him away. No thank you or appreciation or anything.

Once he'd locked the storage closet, he strolled down the hall to get his coat in the staff room. He accidentally/on purpose dropped the envelope, and it popped open, the twist having broken off. Okay, he'd played with it a little on his walk here.

Dean got a glimpse of papers, and a specific drawing caught his attention. It was the fake logo they'd designed to trap their marketing thief. And she'd handed it straight to the president of the company she was betraying.

After shooting off a text to Trey about their culprit, he went in search of Reva. They could finally end this.

She stood in the doorway of the Diamond Ballroom, her smirk unmistakable. He had a feeling that would change soon enough.

Approaching her, he pulled the papers out and held them up. "I'm not sure this is something you should be sharing with anyone else."

Her eyes narrowed and shot daggers at him. "Listen, it's none of your business what I do. You have no idea of the inner workings of this place."

Boy, was she wrong about that. He let her go on with her tantrum.

"Just go bring those like I asked. I paid you your money already. And don't say anything to anyone else. It's nobody else's business."

"You know, you never even said thank you."

Her lips pursed. "I can have you fired if I want. I'm in tight with Demitrius Petrakis."

Dean mumbled, "Not as tight as I am." After taking a deep breath, he straightened and cleared his throat. "You know, my brother always thought highly of you. Why would you do this to him?"

Reva's eyebrows slammed together. "Why do I care what your brother thinks?"

"That Demitrius Petrakis you just mentioned. Sound familiar?"

"What about him?"

"He's my brother."

Her body stiffened. "No. His brother's name is Konstantine. I don't know what you're playing at."

He tapped the name tag on his chest. "Yes, Dean is short for Konstantine."

Her mouth fell open, and her eyes widened.

"You're lying. You can't be Konstantine Petrakis. He lives in New England. He'd never work as a janitor here. He's got millions. What's your angle? You want more money to deliver the envelope? Fine. I'll give you another twenty, but that's it."

"I don't need your money. As you just pointed out, I have millions." He pulled his phone from his pocket and scrolled to a picture of him and his brother together. When he swiveled the screen toward Reva, her face blanched.

"What are you doing here cleaning toilets?"

"Looking for the person who's been selling us out."

A scowl crossed her face, and she shoved her finger at his chest. "Your brother is the one responsible for this. He deserves anything I throw at him. He thinks he can get away with what he's done to me. Well, he can't."

"He gave you this job, even though you didn't have the qualifications. Along with a very healthy salary and bonuses." Reva's paycheck was far higher than Eleni's, and that woman worked her fingers to the bone with this job.

"This job!" Reva's voice rose louder, not caring that people were watching. "I didn't want this job. I wanted to marry him. Be the queen of his empire, not his little tramp whenever he decides to visit. He doesn't appreciate what I could do for him, his image."

"No, I guess he doesn't. Just so you know, these plans are fake. We planted them around to see who the turncoat was."

"If they're fake, then you have nothing against me. Plus, I never actually gave them to anyone."

"Not this time. Who's Bob? I can go ask what his stake in this is. How much are you getting paid to deliver these to The Sands?"

Her lips pressed together, and she shook her head. "Nothing. I haven't gotten a cent. I wanted to pay Demitrius back for the way he's treated me. Bob is a patsy who gives the plans to someone else who works for The Sands. They don't even know who's providing them."

He understood, to a degree, why she was intent on bringing them down. Trey could be a jerk at times when it came to women. Now, what to do with this woman?

"Listen, Reva. I'm sorry that my brother treated you poorly, but what you did can't be overlooked. My suggestion is to leave the island. Don't come back and don't attempt anything else against Yios Corp. If you do, we'll charge you with corporate espionage. I don't think you'll look good in prison stripes."

Her shoulders fell, but her expression softened. "You'd let me just go?"

"If you stay away. No reference from here, though. You understand?"

"Yes, yes, thank you. You are far nicer than your brother. If you ever need anything..." She placed her hands on his shoulders and leaned in. Dean immediately stepped back.

"Don't even try it. I'm not as susceptible as my brother. Just go. Now."

Reva scurried off, heels clicking down the hallway. Luckily, most of the day staff was gone. As he turned to see the few people who'd overheard his conversation, the one person he hadn't wanted stood right there behind him. Eleni.

Her face crumpled, emotions plain to see, then she spun and rushed down the hallway. Dean took off after her. He couldn't let her get away without talking to her.

"Eleni. Let me explain." He darted into the manager's outer office. She had grabbed her bag and was stuffing her purse into it.

"Eleni, look at me."

"I have to go home." She pushed past him to the door.

"You don't get off for a half hour."

She rounded on him and scowled. "I'm sick. My kids are sick. My mother is sick. I need to go. Dock my pay if you need to."

She got as far as the walkway near the tennis courts before he managed to get in front of her and take her arm. She tugged it away immediately.

"So this friendship between us, it was all a ruse? You needed to look like you belonged so you could catch Reva at whatever she was doing?"

"No, Leni. Our friendship was real. That was a bonus."

"A bonus? Like sleeping with me? That's a pretty nice bonus, but I'm not really the millionaire type. Did you enjoy slumming it?"

What was she saying? "I don't understand. You just found out I have millions and you're mad. Most women would be jumping for joy." But Eleni wasn't most women. Something he'd learned during his time here and a reason he loved her.

"You lied to me." Her gaze bore into him like a kick to the groin.

"I told you why I was here."

"You said to check on the resort. And that you were a friend of the family." She crossed her arms over her chest.

He mimicked her stance. "No, you said that." At her disbelieving glare, he continued, "I had to be here without anyone knowing, to catch the traitor who was giving our marketing plans away."

Her eyes narrowed, then got bigger. "Did you think I was involved?"

"I had to consider everyone a suspect at first, but I soon realized there wasn't any way you would have done it. I know how loyal you are, Leni."

He reached out, but she took a step back. "Yet you still didn't tell me. Didn't trust me with your true identity. After all we've done. After all the times you've come to my house for dinner and desserts and playing basketball and going for walks. You didn't trust me." Her voice cracked on the last few words.

"I loved all of those times. They weren't fake for me."

Eleni pressed her lips together and took a step closer. "I haven't had sex since Sean died. I let you get close and trusted you to the point we became intimate. I allowed you in my house and with my kids. They trusted you, and you lied to all of us. Konstantine. Or should I call you Mr. Petrakis now?"

"I was always myself when I was with you and your family. I was able to be simply Dean. Not the CEO of a mega corporation. I appreciated that more than you know."

"Well, I'm glad we could entertain you while you were here undercover. But now you'll be heading back to corporate headquarters and your elite lifestyle."

"Eleni, I—"

"I don't want to see you anymore, *Mr. Petrakis*. Have a nice trip home." She swirled around and almost ran to her car.

Heaving a big sigh, Dean watched as she drove away. A hole the size of a crater opened up in his chest. He needed to talk to her, explain what he'd done and why. *You just did, and she didn't care.* But he hadn't told her he loved her. Would it make a difference at this point?

His phone buzzed, and he swiped it to see a text from Trey. Yeah, he needed to make sure Reva left the island and then head back to Boston for some damage control.

But first he had to go inside and talk to Aarya and Hugh and introduce himself. He'd rather ride a bike over a cliff.

CHAPTER TWENTY

*T*he rain coming down outside mirrored Eleni's mood.

"Mom, is Mr. Dean coming over to watch Star Wars with us today? He said the first one is the best, but I think he meant the fourth one. They did all these movies in a really weird order."

"No, Xander. I told you he had to go back to Boston. That's where his job is. He was only here to help out for a little while." Might as well give them partial truth when the man had lied to them for four months.

Thea pouted. "But he said he'd drive us around to see all the Christmas lights. He thought the ones on the lighthouse would be really cool."

"That's something we always do as a family. We'll go and see them together, just not today when it's raining. They'll look nicer when the sky is clear." They didn't need an interloper horning in on their family traditions. Not that she expected him to show up. He'd left the island the day of the altercation with Reva.

"What about the boat parade, Mom?" Xander asked. "Mr. Dean was really excited about all the lights on the boats as they sailed by the marina. Do you think he forgot? Maybe we should call and remind him."

"Mr. Dean probably has very important things to do at his job, honey. If he really wants to see the boats, I'm sure he'll take the time, but I wouldn't plan on it for now. They aren't until next weekend, so we don't need to worry about it at the moment." Damn the man for making promises to her children and not following through. Damn the man for a lot of things. Most of all for making her fall in love with him.

Thank the good Lord she'd never told him that. Would he have laughed in her face? Or kept it to himself like all his other secrets? He was probably having a good chuckle right now with his wealthy millionaire friends at the yacht club. *Man, you should have seen this cute little secretary I got busy with.* At least she hoped he'd call her cute.

How ridiculous was that? Or the one where she wanted him to come back and tell her he'd fallen in love with her, even though she was a peasant. Ha. She'd been watching too many old movies. She needed to get a grip.

"Get settled in, and I'll make popcorn for the movie."

Thea's eyes bugged out of her head. "Can we eat it in the living room?"

When she nodded, the twins bounced around squealing. It was rare that she let them eat in front of the TV. She didn't have the energy to fight with them today or the heart to say no. Her heart wasn't doing much these days. Oh, it beat its normal rhythm, but there was no leaping for joy when Dean walked by the window and definitely no melting when he held her in his arms and kissed her. It merely did the minimum job to keep her alive.

When the popcorn was ready, she brought the bowl to the kids, then returned to the kitchen to sit at the small breakfast table. Her phone vibrated, and she froze. Dean had been calling and texting for the past four days, since he'd been unmasked. She hadn't responded to either.

"Do you want some tea?" Mom asked as she entered the kitchen.

"*Yes, please,*" she signed back as she answered. Eleni studied her mom as she bustled about the kitchen getting mugs and tea bags and the sugar bowl. Once the tea was ready, Mom brought it to the table and sat across from her.

Pushing a plate of cookies to the middle, Mom said, "Have you heard from Dean?"

The sweets held no appeal for her, since they reminded her too much of that man. "No, Mom. I told you who he really is." Her mom didn't know as many signs and neither did Eleni. She grabbed one of the pads of paper they always had in every room and scribbled what she'd said.

Mom read it and frowned. "Did he tell you he didn't want to see you anymore?"

Eleni shook her head and signed. "*No. I ran away. I didn't want to talk to him.*"

Mom tipped her head, her lips tightening. "Why didn't you give him a chance to explain?"

Eleni grabbed the paper and wrote, *Explain what? That he lied to us the whole time he was here? He doesn't care about us. Everything was a lie.*

"I think he developed feelings for you, sweetie. I know he enjoyed being with the twins. You can't hide that. Maybe you should give him a chance if he calls. I can't believe he just left without a word."

Oh, there'd been many words. Eleni dug her phone from her pocket and scrolled through her messages. She placed the device on the table and spun it so her mom could see.

As Mom read the words, her eyes misted over. Eleni didn't need to look to know what was there. She'd reread them every night as she cried herself to sleep.

She'd tried to take some time off to compose herself, but Aarya had begged her to come in. Reva was gone, and they needed someone to do her job. Hugh was in a snit about the deception Dean had pulled over everyone's eyes, yet he'd been working harder than ever. Aarya hadn't said it, but she got the feeling Hugh's position hinged on him snapping into shape and doing a better job. At least one good thing came of Dean's deception.

Mom tapped the phone and stared at Eleni intently. "These messages don't sound like a man who was only here for a good time. He misses you and the kids. Even me. I have to say I miss him, too. He's become a big part of this family."

Yeah, a millionaire in this family. Wasn't that funny? But when Eleni glanced down and reread how many times Dean had said he missed her, she was far from laughing.

This couldn't be right.

Eleni read through the document again and blinked back tears at the words. Corporate had taken a hand in new programming, and they wanted to roll out a Kids Klub. Had this been Dean's doing? It must be, since so many of the ideas were ones Eleni had told him about.

It didn't look like Eleni would be the one to develop the programs. For now, she was helping out as Activities Director with Reva gone, but Aarya had promised they were advertising for a new one. In the meantime, two college students home on break had shared her old admin assistant duties. Eleni liked the fact it took two people to do what she'd been able to handle by herself. She should never have been given that much to do, but maybe now they'd appreciate her a little more when she went back to her old job.

Did she want to? She'd been enjoying the Activities Director position and the challenges it gave her. The hours were a little different, but it was Christmas break, so homeschooling had taken a holiday as well. Would they even consider her, since she didn't have any background in programming or a degree for it?

"What do you think of the Kids Klub corporate wants rolled out by February?" Aarya poked her head into the office Eleni had been using.

"I love the idea, especially using teachers to run the program. The incentive of a week's free stay at any of the Yios resorts is a nice bonus on top of the pay they'd get."

"I agree." Aarya said and picked up the document with all the changes listed. "I think they'll get some great teachers with that kind of incentive. Thanksgiving break, winter break, some in the spring and summertime. They've even done research into which states have their vacations at what time, so we can promote to those markets. Most likely, we'll need to hire another Activities Director, as well. One for adult activities for the parents who bring their kids to the Klub. Then, one specifically for the Kids Klub."

"It would definitely be more work. Have you had any applicants yet?"

"A few." Aarya nodded, her eyes focused on Eleni. "Mr. Petrakis thought you would be a good fit for the job."

"Mr. Petrakis? Which one?" Had Dean mentioned her and why?

"They both have mentioned what an excellent job you've done here. Konstantine is the one who suggested you could do the programming job. I agree. I think you'd be great."

Eleni shook her head. "I don't have any experience or training in that kind of job."

Aarya laughed. "You're doing it now. And quite well I might add. You don't have to make any decisions now, but you should think about it. We probably won't even start looking at applicants until the new year."

"I'll give it some thought. Thank you, Aarya."

"And don't forget the staff Christmas party tomorrow afternoon."

"How could I forget? So strange that suddenly the bigwigs at corporate want to throw us a huge bash with food and Santa and who knows what else."

"I think the fact Mr. Petrakis spent four months living in our shoes gave him a better idea of what goes on here and the amount of work involved. I definitely heard the word 'bonuses' thrown around. You don't want to miss it. And bring the kids. Santa will be here, and he'll have gifts for them, too."

Aarya left, and Eleni sat back in her chair. Word had come down from corporate to close the restaurant for the afternoon tomorrow. They'd hired off-island caterers to come in and provide food, so the kitchen staff didn't need to work. Santa would be there for the kids, and everyone was expected to make an appearance. The reception desk was even being closed for an hour and staff would be rotated, so all could have time to show up.

Eleni stared out the window at the tennis courts. No one was playing at the moment. Part of the plans for the Kids Klub was to utilize every part of the resort during the off-season months. Like now.

Eleni glanced over the document again, flipping pages to check exactly what was coming. The birthday party weekend package was brilliant. She knew exactly where that had come from.

Using the hair and beauty salon in the hotel for little girls to get done up and all glammed out was straight from the party she'd thrown for Thea, as was using the outdoor areas for any sports parties if that was more to a child's liking. The sunroom could be used for tea parties. The heated pool could host water fun. There were even plans to have a removable roof to keep the pool warmer year-round.

There was a plan to purchase bikes for use by hotel guests for free to avoid the extra cost of renting them. So many new promotions that both integrated families and fun, but also provided some time for kids to go one way and parents to have a little time on their own. The perfect balance for a vacation.

The notation at the bottom about looking into offering scholarships for low-income families, or perhaps even inviting foster children or ones from broken homes who lived in the city the opportunity to spend a week in the fun and sun, made Eleni's heart race.

She bit her lip and stared at her purse. Even after all the texts and calls Dean had sent her, she hadn't responded. They'd slowly dribbled to only a few, but the one this morning had almost made her respond.

Reaching for her phone, she swiped across the screen to read it again.

—*I wish I could show you how much you mean to me. I miss you every second, but I know it's my own fault. I can only say I'm sorry for hurting you. It's the very last thing I'd ever want to do. Maybe someday that huge heart of yours might consider forgiving me.*—

Most of the previous texts and messages were more along the lines of "please, call me," or "let me know you're all right," or "I miss you all." This one touched that broken heart of hers and brought a spark to it again. Maybe what he'd done with the new programming at the resort had played a part in it, too. He'd listened to her, and not in a patronizing way. He'd heard what she'd said and actually considered it. More than considered it. He'd put it into action.

Tapping at the phone, she sent her own message. —*I like the Kids Klub plan.*—

She hadn't forgiven him yet, but this let him know she was at least thinking of him. The phone vibrated seconds after she pressed send.

—*The most incredible, beautiful, intelligent, and loving person came up with the idea.*—

Tears filled her eyes at his words. The mad she'd had inside for the last week started to shrink. It was still there, no doubt, but it didn't seem as strong or hurtful anymore.

—*Sounds like a wonderful person.*—

Okay, so he'd lied to her about who he was. In a way. But he'd lied to everyone not just her...for a reason. She hadn't realized the extent of Reva's anger and deceit. It had cost the resort a great deal of money.

Her phone went off again.

—*She is. You are.*—

Now, he seemed to be making up for what he'd done. Why? To get in her good graces? Because these were solid ideas that could turn a profit? A little of both? Maybe she did need to talk to him and find out exactly what his thoughts were. Too bad he was still in Boston.

—*Thank you.*—

Maybe once Christmas was over, she could take a few days off and bring the kids to Boston. They'd never seen snow. It might be fun. The extra she'd gotten in this week's paycheck would cover some of the cost. They could eat grilled cheese and tomato soup for a month to pay off the rest. Dean could hardly blow her off with Thea and Xander by her side. His words made her think he wouldn't. The least she could do was to listen to him.

CHAPTER TWENTY-ONE

"**H**o, ho, ho, Merry Christmas!"

Dean felt like he'd said that about a billion times today. For some reason, it didn't bother him. He'd had kids on his lap for the past hour and had heard all sorts of wishes coming from them. The kids he really wanted to see hadn't shown up yet. His nerves shook at the thought they might not come.

But Eleni had texted him back yesterday. She hadn't said she forgave him or wanted to see him, but she'd finally responded after more than a week of radio silence. His ulcer had gone into overdrive, the one that had all but gone away when he'd been plain old Dean Peters in maintenance.

This island had been good for his anxiety. The island and the people on it. Particularly one family. He'd asked Aarya to make sure Eleni, Georgie, and the kids came today, but there was only so much the manager could do. Going to a party wasn't really in Eleni's job description. Dean was hoping to give her a completely different job that didn't involve the resort, if only he could get her alone for a few minutes.

His eyes lingered on Hugh, who was aware his days at the resort were most likely numbered, as the man nodded at guests but didn't interact much. It had been fun seeing the assistant manager squirm when he'd shed his fake identity.

Dean had taken a deep breath as he'd entered the admin office, when what he'd really wanted to do was run after Eleni. She'd been clear that she wanted no part of him. Aarya had come out of her office and glanced around.

"Did Eleni leave already?"

"I'm afraid so. She wasn't feeling well."

Hugh grunted from his doorway. "I didn't have any peanuts today, so don't blame me."

"Actually, I have to talk to both of you about something important."

Aarya stood up straight while Hugh leaned against the door frame and rolled his eyes. "You're quitting? Well, no tears from me."

"I'm not, but Reva won't be working here any longer. I fired her."

Hugh finally straightened up, his face red. "Who do you think you are? You work in maintenance, not in administration. This is grounds for *you* to be dismissed. Agreed, Aarya?"

The manager narrowed her eyes. "Mr. Peters?"

Dean had taken his wallet from his pocket and opened to where his license was. Aarya's mouth dropped open, but then she smirked.

Dean held it so Hugh could see. The man froze, then his eyes flipped back and forth from Dean to Aarya. "Did you know?"

Aarya chuckled. "No, but I am curious, Mr. Petrakis. Is there a reason you came here undercover?"

"Someone's been stealing marketing ideas and giving them to The Sands. I needed to find out who."

Holding his hands up, Hugh squeaked, "It wasn't me."

"I know. It was Reva. That's why she no longer works here."

Hugh's face turned crimson, and he stared at the floor. Was he waiting for Dean to fire him, too? It might come to that, but for now he'd leave it alone.

"In the time I've been here, I've also noted a number of areas that could use improvement. I assume I'll have complete cooperation from both of you going forward with these projects."

"Of course. I'd love to hear what you observed. I can imagine administration doesn't always see the whole picture." Aarya smiled, and Dean loved that she took it all in stride.

Hugh, on the other hand, was a mass of nerves, suddenly falling all over himself trying to please Dean. It had been humorous to see. At the time.

Dean now scanned the restaurant as Trey mingled with the staff and handed out the bonuses they'd hinted at. Each of the employees smiled with thanks, then wandered away to open the envelope. The looks on their faces when they saw what was in it was magical. Most of them ran back over to Trey, shaking his hand exuberantly with even more thanks.

Even though it had been Dean's idea for the bonuses, he hadn't wanted the credit. Trey had always been the face of Yios, there was no reason for them to change things now. As it was, most of the people here had no idea who was in the Santa suit.

"Hi, Santa. Jimena would love to come talk to you." It was Maria, the housekeeping staff he'd helped after the rich party boys had destroyed the room. She had a little girl with her who couldn't be more than four.

"Hey there, Jimena. Would you like to tell me what you want for Christmas?"

Jimena nodded shyly and took a tentative step closer. Dean held out his hand and waited.

Maria held the girl's arm and nodded. "It's okay. I'll be right here."

Jimena approached, and Dean leaned forward. "Is there something special you'd like?" He tried to remember what she'd asked for. He'd tasked Aarya with finding out what the kids of the staff had on their list that the parents couldn't afford. She'd done it under the guise that her husband's company had gotten tons of donations and wanted to parcel out the items.

The girl nodded and suddenly Dean remembered. "I bet you'd like a toy puppy that barks and waggles his tail."

Jimena's eyes popped open. "I do want that. How did you know?"

"Santa knows everything. If you go over to that elf near the table and tell her your name, I think she might have something for you."

One of the college students home for the holidays was manning the table with the gifts. She'd been paying attention and already had Jimena's present in her hand. There were only a few presents left.

Maria nodded. "Thank you so much for everything. Not just the present for my daughter but for what you did for me and all of the staff here."

Apparently, not everyone was fooled by the costume. The beard didn't completely hide his scar.

As Jimena and Maria proceeded to the table, Dean's attention turned to the door again. Xander and Thea strolled in, holding hands with their grandmother. Had Eleni not come? His heart hurt thinking he'd never talk to her again.

The twins ran toward him, and he shifted in his seat.

"Ho, ho, ho, Merry Christmas. Would you like to sit on Santa's lap and tell him what you want?"

They both came over and each settled on a knee.

"I really want a scooter." Xander went first. "One that has lights that glow when it rolls. I know my mom doesn't have the money for that, though. Maybe you could help her out."

"Hmm. A scooter, huh? What about you?" He focused on Thea.

Thea's mouth turned down, and she sniffed. "I just want you to come back with us, so Mama doesn't cry as much anymore."

So much for anonymity. "Your mom's been crying?"

Xander rolled his eyes. "She'd be mad if she knew we said anything. But she misses you. We miss you, too. Are you gonna come back to the island?"

"I'd like to. I miss all of you, as well, but I had to do some work at the corporate office in Boston. And figure out a few other things."

Thea leaned in for a hug. "We want you to be here with us. If I give you my special pink shell, the one you thought was really pretty, would you come back?"

"I'll give you *all* my shells," Xander added, his eyes pleading.

God, he'd missed these kids.

"Thanks. I appreciate the offer. The thing is your mom's a little upset that I didn't tell her exactly who I was."

"But you're rich. I don't know why she doesn't get excited about that," Xander huffed.

"Because money isn't important to your mother. Not in the way it is to some people. She's right. There are things far more important than wealth."

"Like family and love," Thea whispered as she nestled on his shoulder.

Dean chuckled. "See, your mom taught you well. Now, I just need to make her see how much I care about her. And you and your grandmother, too. Maybe you can help me, so I can get her alone to do that."

The twins grinned, and they chatted about exactly what they'd do. Just as they jumped off his lap, Eleni entered the room, and Dean couldn't do anything except stare. How had she gotten more beautiful in only two weeks?

"You two, head over to the table and the elf will give you your presents. Then, I need to give your mom hers."

Laughing, they trotted over, and Dean checked to see if all the gifts had been claimed. The elf nodded and gave him a thumbs up. Xander's squeal as he opened up the scooter could be heard throughout the room. It wasn't the first happy yell tonight.

Dean signaled his brother, who'd just approached Eleni with her bonus envelope. Her expression showed her awareness of who Trey was. Then, her head whipped around, her eyes searching. For him?

Eleni stepped through the door of the Black Pearl and glanced around for her family. With all the staff members being here at once, parking was severely limited, and she'd needed to park on the road once she'd dropped Xander, Thea, and her mom at the door. She hadn't wanted the kids walking on the road with the extra cars on the island. Tonight was when the Festival of Lights had the boat parade. It would be packed.

The kids sat on Santa's lap, most likely giving him a list of toys she couldn't afford. They'd already gone over what they'd most likely get, and she had a nice toy for each of the kids that would be from Santa.

An attractive, dark-haired man with an olive complexion strolled toward her, and her heart skipped a beat for a second. It wasn't Dean, but now that she saw Demitrius Petrakis again, she could see the resemblance between the two.

"Eleni Griffin?" Demitrius asked, holding out his hand. "You're the only one who hasn't gotten your bonus check yet."

So the rumor was true. "Yes, I am. Sorry, the parking outside is full, and I had to put my car down the road." The real reason they were later was her stomach being in knots thinking Dean might be here. But she didn't see him anywhere. Had he seriously not shown up, after the many texts saying he missed her?

"I'm Demitrius Petrakis. You can call me Trey."

He certainly hadn't offered that familiarity the last time she'd met him. Had something changed? Did he know her relationship with his brother?

"Thank you. It's very kind of Yios Corp. to throw this party."

"Trying to show our appreciation for all that you do. Aarya tells me you're indispensable."

Eleni shrugged. "I'm just doing my job like everyone else."

Trey glanced over his shoulder at Santa, then tipped his head. "Guess I need to do mine now. It was lovely meeting you again, Eleni."

Had he actually remembered meeting her the first time? She doubted it. The man sauntered over to where Santa held a microphone. Trey took it and gave it a tap.

The crowd quieted down and faced the two men.

"Merry Christmas, everyone. For those who don't know, I'm Demitrius Petrakis, co-owner and CFO of Yios Corporation, the company that runs The Ocean Pearl Resort. Also, the one who signed those Christmas bonus checks you all have in your hands. And even though you all thanked me quite nicely, I have to confess, it wasn't my idea. I've enjoyed meeting all of you, but now I want to hand over the stage to my brother, Konstantine Petrakis. Maybe you can go find him for us, Santa."

Eleni's insides did a little jig, and her nerves exploded. Where was Dean?

Santa stepped off the platform and slipped behind a screen. As he walked away, Eleni recognized those long trim legs in the black pants and the slight limp. A few seconds later, Dean appeared from behind the partition. The coat, hat, and fake beard had been removed. There were a few gasps from the crowd. Many had heard the stories, but not everyone believed them.

Dean took the microphone, and she could tell from the way he stood, he was uneasy.

"Hey there, folks. Most of you know me as Dean Peters, and for four long months I was. While I'm still Dean in every way, except my present job description, I now have a greater appreciation for what you do here. Because of you, Yios makes an incredible profit every year. It didn't seem right that managers and administration are the only ones to benefit from this as you're the ones doing the hard work. The bonus you got today is only a small example of what we're sharing with you. Trey and I will be going over each job position and salary and making necessary changes. For the better."

A round of applause echoed through the room, and Dean's face flushed. He glanced around and his gaze fell on her. The expression on his face spoke volumes, but Eleni didn't want to interpret it yet.

"Along with new pay scales and added staffing for positions that are overworked, we're rolling out some new programming. It was brought to my attention that during the winter months the resort is underused, which would be a perfect time to allow families to enjoy during vacations. We'll be adding a Kids Klub with activities for both children and their parents. We're also looking into scholarships for underprivileged children and those in foster care. We'll be ramping up precautions for those with allergies and disabilities, as well. We want to encourage all staff to voice their opinions on any matter and will set up ways to report problems that arise. Ways in which you can remain anonymous, if you choose."

More applause broke out across the room, and tears sprang to Eleni's eyes. This was the generous man she'd fallen in love with. The one who'd helped her with so much and taken the time to play with her kids and get to know them.

Dean waved his hand around the room. "There's plenty of food, so help yourself. The boat parade starts once it gets dark. I'd like to invite you to stick around here and watch it from either the dock or the beach in front of the resort. Arrangements have been made to transport anyone home if they've had too much to drink. Please, take us up on that offer. Merry Christmas."

Another cheer went up, then the staff began chattering again while filling their plates. Eleni's eyes never left Dean. He placed the microphone on a table and headed in her direction. Eleni froze. What would she say to him?

With so many employees stopping him to talk or thank him, it took forever for him to arrive. Eleni didn't move from her spot. When he finally reached her, his face was tight and anxious.

"Hey, Leni. How are you?"

She wasn't sure how to put into words all she was feeling. "This is quite a party. The staff will be talking about it for a while."

"The only one of the staff I have any interest in at the moment is you. Can we talk?"

She nodded, not sure her vocal chords were working right.

His gaze searched left and right, then he reached for her hand. "Not here. Let me get Georgie and the kids settled with Trey."

Her stomach flipped when she placed her hand in his, but the smile and relief on his face brought her back to reality. Would this work out for them? Would she get a happily ever after like in a fairy tale, or would everything crash and burn like it had in the past?

Dean motioned her mother and the kids over to where Trey stood and introduced them all.

"I'm taking Eleni out for a little while. We'll be back in time for the boat parade. I promise." He signed to her mom, and Eleni's heart melted again. "Eat all the food. We don't want any left over."

Xander high fived Dean while Thea sidled close to Eleni and hugged her. The girl tipped her face up and whispered, "Mom, we really miss Dean, so if he wants to come back, will you let him? Please?"

Eleni hugged her daughter, knowing she wasn't the only one who had hopes and dreams. "I'll see what happens." She kissed Thea's head, then followed Dean from the room.

Once outside, he led her to his old beat-up truck. "You still have this? I expected some fancy sports car."

His grin sent shivers through her. "I have one of those, too, but I kind of got used to this one. Is it okay for now? I can bring out the BMW another time."

Eleni let him help her into the passenger seat, then she fiddled with the seat belt while he climbed behind the wheel. Soon, they were crossing the island and heading toward the lighthouse. Her hands clenched together to keep them from shaking, and not because of the chilly night air. It had warmed up today into the sixties, but by the ocean it was always a few degrees lower.

They pulled into the lighthouse parking lot, and Dean killed the engine. "Let's walk on the beach for a bit, if that's okay?"

"Sure." She got herself out of the truck before he could come around and darted toward the sand. He caught up with her a minute later.

They walked in silence at first, and Eleni didn't know if she should say something or not. Dean's gaze ping-ponged all over the place, and he kept taking deep breaths like he was about to start speaking. Was he nervous? Just because he was the head of a large corporation didn't mean he was extroverted. When he was Dean Peters, he rarely spoke to anyone if he didn't need to. Her included. At first. He'd eventually come around. Thea and Xander hadn't really given him any choice.

"Thank you for all the bonuses for the staff. I know lots of them could really use the extra money. Did you do that because of me?"

His head whipped toward her. "What? No. I did it because I spent too much time cleaning up vomit and spilled food. No one should do that job for under a million a year. Unfortunately, we can't really afford that kind of pay, but I'm hoping the little raise we gave will help."

Eleni slipped her hand through his elbow and hugged it. He took another deep breath, but this time his shoulders dropped down instead of clinging to the side of his neck.

Lights shone brightly up ahead, and Eleni halted her steps. "Looks like someone's in The Hideaway. Ben Hadley told me they've been working night and day to get it fixed up."

"Do you want to take a peek?"

Eleni grinned. "Only if no one's there. I don't see any vehicles in the driveway."

They jogged faster up between the sea grass and under the trees. The porch wasn't sagging anymore, and it had been freshly painted. The entire house had new siding with gorgeous cedar shingles in a light washed-out gray. White Christmas lights outlined the house and the porch, and wreaths decorated each window.

"Oh, Dean, look how beautiful it is. Like it's been given a second chance."

"I like the idea of second chances. Do you think you could give me one?"

He sounded so forlorn, she hugged his arm tighter and moved in to kiss it. His other hand held up a set of keys.

"What are those?"

"The keys to your new house." His brows rose up.

"My new..." Had he just said what she thought? And why wasn't she exploding with joy? "I think we need to roll back a few steps to talking about us first."

"Is there an us? I tried talking to you before, but you wouldn't respond." Dean scowled, then stared at his feet.

"You lied to me. To us. My mother and my kids. It hurts that you didn't trust me."

"I know, and I'll be forever sorry about that."

"Why didn't you tell me?"

Shoving his hands in his pockets, Dean rocked back on his feet. "Because I was undercover, trying to figure out—"

"No, I know why you originally didn't tell me, and I understand that. But once we started hanging out and kissing and...other things. You still didn't tell me."

His hands emerged from his pockets, and he cupped her face. "I wasn't sure how you felt about me yet. I was afraid if I told you, you'd be mad. Like you were. Are. I thought if I bought you The Hideaway and fixed it up, you'd see how much I cared for you."

Eleni took a step back. "You really think that a house is more important than telling me the truth? Do you really not know me at all?"

The wind whipped up, and Dean forked his fingers through his hair, pushing it back. "All my life, the people who seemed to care about me did it because of the money my family had. As I got older, it never changed. Women wanted to go out with me for what I could give them. I'd overheard one of my steady girlfriends say she put up with my scars and limp because I could buy her anything. She could stay at a different resort every month if she wanted. Since I was a workaholic, she could even have her fun with other guys, and I'd probably never even notice."

Crossing her arms over her chest, Eleni frowned. "You thought I was like those women? That I'd only like you because of your money? I never even knew about it, and I still liked you. More than liked you." She wouldn't say it yet. Couldn't tell him how much she cared, if what was between them ended up bent and broken.

"I knew soon after I met you that you didn't care about money, not in the same way any of my old girlfriends did. The more I hung around, the more I realized you liked Dean Peters regardless of how much I was worth. I just still couldn't bring myself to tell you. Not the complete truth. I made an attempt the night at the Captain's Table."

"I'll give you that one." He had made an effort. It still hurt that he didn't trust her enough for the entire truth.

"I kept thinking what if you'd simply been having fun at my expense. I needed to be absolutely certain it was me, Dean, that you cared for."

"But you aren't Dean Peters. You're Konstantine Petrakis."

He shook his head. "The funny thing is the longer I stayed on the island, the more I knew I was really Dean. I felt more comfortable in his shoes than I'd ever felt as Konstantine. And that's who fell in love with you. Dean."

"Fell in love with me?" Had he seriously said it or was she hallucinating?

He picked up her hands and kissed her knuckles. "I love you, Eleni. I haven't been this happy in I don't know how long. Being with you and your mom and the kids has brought such joy to my life I've never experienced before. You not only brought me out of my shell, you cracked it so I don't ever want to go back there. Unless you won't forgive me."

Stepping into his arms, she pressed a kiss to his chin. "Yes, I forgive you. I don't know how it is to be rich, but I can imagine it's trying at times."

"Would you like to try it? I can show you the house."

"You really bought it?" Tears welled in her eyes.

He shook the keys and led her up the back deck. Inside, her mind practically exploded with how perfect it was. The kitchen appliances and floor. The living room was empty with only some painting cloths bunched in a corner, but the walls had been redone and the woodwork sanded and refinished.

"They aren't quite done, but I couldn't wait any longer to show you."

"It's perfect. The color is exactly what I wanted."

"The kitchen's only pale yellow. I figured you could add the navy accents yourself. Let me show you upstairs. I had to ask at the hardware store about sage and periwinkle."

As they trotted up the stairs, she shouted back, "What color did you go with?"

"You'll see."

She slipped into the main bedroom and switched on the light. "Sage. Oh, it's as beautiful as I thought it would be."

"I personally liked it better than purple. You know, in case I ever get a chance to visit here. I've got some furniture coming soon, and I didn't do any curtains or stuff like that. I thought you'd want to do all that yourself."

Eleni peeked in the other rooms, then twirled in the hallway between them.

Dean held out the keys. "Regardless, the house is yours."

She tilted her head. "Regardless of what?"

"This." He held out a box and flipped the lid. "I didn't think anyone would ever love me for who I am and not for my money. You did. And your family did. Before you even knew who I was, you gave me the best of yourself and shared your family with me. Made me realize how much I missed out with them and helped me remember what it was like to be a kid again."

The ring was gorgeous. Not as big and gaudy as she figured a millionaire would buy. Dainty, feminine, but still lots of diamonds.

"I love you, Leni. I want to love you forever and be your husband. I want to help raise your children in the same loving way you have. Will you give me the chance?"

There wasn't even any hesitation. Her head bobbed up and down. "Yes. I'll marry you. I love you, Dean. Because you're a good person, and I know you'll be a fabulous husband and father to my kids."

His arms enclosed her, and their lips met. Hers had been bereft without his ever since he'd left. "Won't it be awkward with you as my boss? Will that cause problems?"

Dean pressed a kiss to her nose. "That was something else I wanted to discuss. Reassigning you to a different job."

"You mean the Activities Director?"

"I was thinking more along the lines of my wife and my adviser. You can focus on teaching the kids and not worry about leaving them during the day. Unless you really want to have a job outside the home."

The thoughts swirled through her mind and so many scenarios presented themselves. "Maybe someday when the kids are older, I'd love to work more closely at the resort. But for now, if you're okay with it, I'd love to spend more time with Thea and Xander."

His face moved in for a kiss. "And me?"

"Oh, yes. Most definitely you."

EPILOGUE

"**I**s Mr. Petrakis in?" Eleni asked Dean's secretary, Maggie. The woman had been thrilled to be transferred from cold Boston to somewhere much warmer in the winter.

"Yes, Mrs. Petrakis. He's always here for you. Go on in."

Eleni still gave a tiny knock on the door, in case he was on the phone or in the middle of something.

Dean glanced up from his computer screen, and a grin split his face. He waved her in, so she closed the door behind her and crossed the room. Dean's new fourth floor office in the back of the financial suite had come out great.

As she stepped onto the balcony that looked out on the beach, she chuckled at Nadine with the four kids. They still took turns with homeschooling, even though she'd given up her full-time job here. Dean eased up behind her, enveloped her in his arms, and kissed her neck. He'd sure learned exactly what set her off in the past few months that they'd been married.

"To what do I owe this pleasure, Leni?"

The pleasure she was getting from those talented lips on her shoulder should have been enough reason.

"I was downstairs helping to train the two new admin assistants and figured I'd see if you had time to have lunch with your wife."

"I always have time for my wife. Did you bring something, or should we see what Vlad has cooked up today?"

"I asked him to send something up. It'll be here soon."

"How are the ladies working out in the manager's office?"

Dean settled into the chair on the balcony and drew her into his lap. She'd never get enough of his love and attention.

"They're doing great, as is the new assistant manager. It's a shame Hugh left the company."

Since Dean had shown up to run Yios Corp. from The Ocean Pearl, Hugh had decided he needed a change in scenery. Eleni couldn't complain. They'd hired someone for his job, plus two new activity directors, one for the Kids Klub and one for the adults and family activities. Eleni had been working with them on the new programming. It was nice to have a flexible schedule with less hours each week and much of it she could do from home.

They'd moved into The Hideaway last month after their wedding. Then, Dean had taken all of them, the kids and her mother included, to Greece for their honeymoon. They'd visited her mom's old village and met many relatives, then traveled to see where Dean's family was from. They'd spent another week at the Yios resort on Mykonos, enjoying the amenities and the special attention they got from being Konstanine Petrakis' family.

Back home, her mom was over the moon, loving how she could watch the waves roll in and out every day. The kids enjoyed being on the beach and especially the puppy Dean had gotten them. Eleni had been somewhat miffed at the suggestion, but Thea was extremely responsible in walking and feeding the animal, and Dean had picked up any slack. Eleni hadn't had to do much besides play with the "real" Cuddles when she wanted to.

Vlad spent a good deal of time at the house with them and had asked Mom to help him in the Ocean Pearl kitchen, making and testing new recipes. She'd been thrilled, and Eleni had a feeling there might come a time when her mother would leave them. Vlad had become quite vocal in how much he cared for the woman.

As she snuggled into Dean's arms, he stroked her face. "Are you happy, Mrs. Petrakis?"

"I am. Never happier. I wasn't sure I'd get this second chance after Sean died. But here you are, making my dreams come true. I love every minute of being with you."

"I love you, Leni. I always will."

Seems the Legend of Last Chance Beach had struck again.

Take a sneak peek at the next book in the Last Chance Beach Romance series by Kari Lemor, *Masquerade Under the Moon.* Trey Petrakis' story.

Masquerade Under the Moon

Destiny Fortunato held up the mulberry chiffon material and shook her head. "I don't think so. There isn't enough here to cover a freckle."

Her roommate and fellow teacher, Cheri Townsend, laughed. "That's the point, Desi. You got such an amazing tan this summer; you need to show it off."

Destiny eyed the costume and glared at her friend. They'd been rooming together at the exclusive Ocean Pearl Resort on Last Chance Beach all summer. It had been an unbelievable experience working at the new Klub Kid that the resort started this year.

"I shouldn't go to the masquerade party tonight. I'm scheduled to work." She cleared her throat, but it still held a raspy tone from the salt water she'd swallowed this afternoon when one of the kids had pushed her under the waves.

Cheri flopped back on her bed. "You've been putting in a ton of extra hours and changing shifts with many of the Klub staff. Especially me. I owe you."

"You just want to hang out with Dana now that the two of you have discovered your mutual attraction. Don't deny it."

"I'm not denying anything. It's great hanging with Dana, and we want as much time together before the summer ends. We all go home tomorrow. However, it's not like we can make out in front of the kids."

"I don't know." Destiny held up the gold chains and bangles that went with the rest of the outfit.

Cheri jackknifed to a sitting position and scowled. "It's your thirtieth birthday for Pete's sake. You need to live a little. Have some fun."

"I've had lots of fun this summer."

One eyebrow rose. Cheri's pale skin had been slathered in SPF five thousand during their time here. "Fun with the kids. It's not the same as adult fun. I'm happy to finally pay you back for switching all those shifts with me. Take advantage of it."

"All the parents will be at the party. Won't they think it's strange my being there?"

Shooting off the bed, Cheri dug underneath and pulled out a mask. "They won't even know it's you in this."

Destiny gawked at the gorgeous item. Gold plated and dotted with multi-colored gems, it took her breath away. The size of it would cover half her face. From her nose to her forehead, anyway, leaving only her lips visible. Could she do this?

She picked up the costume, shades of Scheherazade, and gathered her courage. It was her birthday, and she deserved to have some fun. Who would know? The party was open to the public, and the owners, Konstantine Petrakis and his wife, Eleni, had encouraged any of the staff who weren't working to attend if they wanted.

Destiny was so thankful for the opportunity to work here this summer after the mess she'd made of her last job. Pushing that disaster to the back of her mind, she smiled at how great it had been on Last Chance Beach. It was a low-key island vacation spot that also had plenty of tourist attractions. And more on the way, she'd been told. Some of the locals weren't thrilled with the development, while others loved seeing more tourist money being poured into the community. Since Destiny's job was ending tomorrow, it didn't matter to her.

"So you're gonna do it? Go to the party? I heard the other Mr. Petrakis is going to be there. Play your cards right and maybe you can stay here for good. It's a beautiful location."

Destiny cringed. "Demitrius, the playboy? Why in the world would I even care about meeting him? I'm aware of his reputation, and he's the last man I'd ever want to get involved with."

Cheri bundled her in a hug. "I know that no-good assistant principal used you and tossed you aside like a dirty tissue, but you can't let it color the rest of your life."

Destiny squeezed back, then released her friend. "I won't, but I also won't get involved with anyone I work for again, especially someone with a reputation as a love 'em and leave 'em kind of guy. Now, let's get me decked out in this costume, so you can get to the kids. You've got to be in the Klub room thirty minutes before the party begins."

The two of them giggled like schoolgirls as she donned the small satin vest that hugged her B cups, pushing them up to appear larger. The fact the front fabric didn't touch and was only held together by a few small metal closures made Destiny feel decadent and inordinately sexy. Something she'd never considered herself before. She was an elementary schoolteacher and had to maintain a certain professional persona. In public, anyway.

The teeny bikini-like bottom made her gasp. However, the skirt with the swirling layers of scarves covered most of her bottom and legs, unless she spun around, which she did in front of the mirror just to see what others would see.

"*Bellissimo*. Not too shabby," as her nonna would say.

"Girl, you are stunning. Gorgeously tanned skin, long legs and arms. Tiny waist, curvy hips and top. You'll have every guy there tripping over himself to be with you."

Destiny rolled her eyes. "Many of the guys there are married. Hopefully, they won't be tripping anywhere."

"Sure, some of the Klub parents are married, but a bunch of guys are still here from that wedding two days ago. Go a little wild tonight. Have some grown-up fun. I'll even make you a deal. Dana's roommate left early today. I'll stay there, and you can have this room to yourself."

"I'm not a one-night stand kind of girl, Cher. But I will go and flirt and dance and have some fun. I promise."

Once she'd slipped her feet into the soft gold shoes, she examined herself in the mirror. The wig with the long, dark, curly hair changed her entire appearance. Cheri had outlined her eyes in smoky grays and blues and attached false eyelashes. The deep burgundy lipstick was applied to enlarge her mouth and form a sexy bow. Holy cow. She'd never looked like this before.

Turning one way, then the other, Destiny peeked at all the exposed skin. The bangles on her wrists jangled, as well as the row of coins that hung from her neck and waist. More gold coins hung from the twisted scarf that surrounded her head. On her ears hung large gold loops.

"Put these on, too." Cheri clasped wide metal cuffs to her upper arms, then attached anklets that also made noise.

"Everyone will hear me coming, that's for sure." Destiny did a little hip wiggle, then held her hands up, twisting them seductively like she'd seen belly dancers do. This could be so much fun.

"Now to add the mask." Cheri placed it on her face and wove the string through the wig before she tied it. "That should keep it from falling off."

The reflection in the mirror was someone Destiny didn't know. Her Italian heritage and the summer sun had helped darken her normally lighter skin. The physical activity she'd done with the children had toned up every visible ounce of her. Not bad for an old schoolteacher of thirty.

"You're sure?" she asked one last time.

Cheri narrowed her eyes and growled. "This is your time to do anything you want to do. No one will even recognize you in that get up."

Anything she wanted to do. Sounded great. Too bad she was practical, reliable, conservative Destiny. Swiveling in the mirror this way and that, she had to admit she looked hot. For one night, she could become someone completely different. Not that she'd go off and hook up with a guy, but she could have some fun with the single ones there. Maybe even a few. Who would know?

If someone somehow figured out it was her, what was the worst that could happen? They didn't invite her back to teach at Klub Kid during the next vacation week. However, the owners had made it a point to invite any staff not working tonight to come and have a good time.

A good time. That's what she'd have.

Make sure to check out Trey and Destiny's story in Masquerade Under the Moon.

https://www.karilemor.com/masquerade-under-the-moon

Find all Kari's books here: https://www.karilemor.com/

Kari's mailing list - News and special deals, sometimes freebies! https://www.karilemor.com/

Join her Reader's Group -The Lit Lounge - for fun and first- hand friendship:

https://www.facebook.com/groups/373521153021256

Here's where you can connect with her on social media

facebook.com/Karilemorauthor

twitter.com/karilemor

instagram.com/karilemorauthor

pinterest.com/karilemor

bookbub.com/authors/kari-lemor

Made in the USA
Monee, IL
28 September 2023

43635366R00134